Ivy Moon

Last Girl on Earth

W.C. Furney

Ivy Moon

Last Girl on Earth

Black Hearts Publishing
www.billfurney.com

Ivy Moon Last Girl on Earth is a work of great fiction. All incidents and dialogue, and all characters except public figures, are products of the author's vivid imagination. Where real public figures appear or are mentioned, the situations, incidents, and dialogues about those persons are entirely fictional. In all other respects, any resemblance to actual persons, living or dead, events, is entirely coincidental.

Credits

Cover Photography..................Jeanette Canady Furney
Moon Photo......................Ganapathy Kumar/Unsplash
Cover Models... ....Sophie Sullivan
Finlay Furney
Creative Consultants.........................Rachael M. Weber
Raelyn M. Weber
Ryliegh M. Weber
Graphic Art Adviser............................Meredith Walsh
Beekeeping Adviser............................Janelle Williams
Pharmaceutical Adviser......Myndi Morrison Fitzgerald
Nautical Adviser...................................Les Pendleton
Proofreading..................................Melanie Galloway

First Edition

ISBN-13: 978-0-9988921-3-9
ISBN: 0-9988921-3-0

This novel is dedicated to Jeanette, my love, my wife, mother of our children, partner, counselor, muse, and writer's widow...without whom none of this would have been possible. Thank you for putting up with me despite me being me.

Table of Contents

The Ivy Moon rolls in at the end of the harvest season. Ivy often lives on after its host plant has died – a reminder to us that life goes on in the endless cycle of life, death, and rebirth. The Celts called this month Gort (go-ert). This is a time to banish the negative from your life, do workings related to improving yourself, and placing a barricade between you and the things that are toxic to you. Ivy can be used in magic performed for healing, protection, cooperation, and to bind lovers together.

...MULTIPLE SOURCES

I am

"My name is Ivy Moon," I say to Tonka. He stares at me with dark, intense eyes. Biding his time. Waiting for me to make a move. "It's the name I've given myself. The kitchen calendar has all the dates in September marked off except for the thirtieth, so I think it's today's date. It's a Celtic Tree Calendar, and it shows today is the first day of the Ivy Moon. I can't remember my real name, so I'm going with that. Do you like it?"

Tonka shifts his weight from one side to the other, unimpressed. His eyes glance at my hands like he's expecting me to use sign language. But I don't know sign language. I don't even know how old I am.

"Maybe fifteen," I say, as though he'd asked. "Maybe sixteen. I feel sixteen, but it's only a guess. There's no way to know for sure."

Tonka cuts me a look that says, "That's nice, but who cares?" Then sits on the floor, waiting.

"But I'm getting ahead of myself. A good story should start at the beginning, so...

"My first memory is of this morning. The pungent odors of mold and mildew assaulted my nose, and when I opened my eyes, I found myself on the cabin floor of the sailboat outside your house. I must have rolled out of the berth when the boat listed against the steps. Faint light was shining through the portholes, so it was hard to see. There was an irregular clanging sound, like a bell ringing in the distance. Familiar yet out of place. Curious and confused, I found my way to the hatchway to go on deck.

"The boat was listing to the starboard side, making the hatch difficult to open. When I managed to lock it in place, I crawled outside to see the world for the first time. That's when my life began.

"Dark, heavy clouds blanketed the sky and a gale-force wind wailed around me. The only sound I could hear above the constant howl was the halyard banging against the aluminum mast like a dinner bell...the source of the familiar sound.

"How do I know what a halyard is? Or the difference between starboard and port? I don't know. I have no memories of sailing. I can't remember any personal details about myself. I'm a newborn with no past, only awareness. But more about that in a minute.

"To the portside lay an open expanse of cattails, a marsh, flooded by the waning storm. The receding floodwaters...heavy with earthy marshland scents...reached halfway up the stalks. Their brown oblong heads had only recently emerged from the water. At the flood's peak, the tall grass stalks were completely covered by water.

"When I turned to look at the starboard side, I couldn't believe my eyes. The boat was resting against a house! Well, not against the house, exactly. It was a wide, steep set of steps leading up to an elevated back porch. One banister was so close I could have leaned out over the deck's lifeline and touched it.

"The house...which sits atop tall pylons...still had two or three feet of water underneath it. The boat had followed the stair's banisters down as the water receded. When the hull hit bottom, the boat began leaning toward the house. That's why I fell out of the berth."

Tonka looks at me with a blank expression, which I take to be disbelief.

"Scared? Of course," I say, louder than I intended. "To be honest, I was on the verge of panic. But then a voice spoke to me. You know, from inside. It kept saying, 'Everything will be all right...you can work it out.' I figured, if a voice in my head believes in me, who am I to argue? So, taking a deep breath, I climbed off the boat onto the steps. Bad move!

"The effort made me dizzy just as a big gust of wind hit me. I lost my balance and fell into the water. The outflowing current pulled me toward the open water. I swam as hard as I could, but made no headway. If I didn't make it back, I was certain to drown.

"Again, I fought off the panic. I don't know how I made it. The anchor line had broken free. Maybe I grabbed it and pulled myself in hand over hand. It's all a blank to me because I passed out.

"The next thing I remember is being inside the screened porch at the top of the steps. The wind was still blowing like crazy and I struggled to gather myself. I sat up and looked around, hoping to spot someone or something that might help. I could see a house next door, but no lights or any signs of people. On the other side is a wooded lot and maybe a house beyond. It was impossible to tell. If so, it didn't have lights either.

A big gust of wind buffets the house and the windows rattle. The Westie jumps up and growls.

"It's OK," I say, "It's just the storm."

Tonka growls again, then sits down, ready to hear the rest of my story.

"At least it's good to know I'm in some kind of neighborhood," I continue. "The power is out, so I'm sure people are hunkered down in their homes. Or maybe they evacuated before the storm. If so, they're sure to return once the weather clears. I'll just stay here until then.

"Anyway, as I was saying, having caught my breath, I began checking out the house. I knocked on one of the glass doors to the porch, hoping someone might be home despite it being dark inside. No one answered, so I knocked again just to be safe.

"That's when you ran into the room, barking and growling. Your message was clear. 'This is my home and I will defend it to the death!'

"I don't mean to hurt your feelings, and I admire your bravery, but Westies aren't the most terrifying breed of dogs, you know? So, I tested the door and found it wasn't locked. When I stepped inside, you stopped barking and sniffed my ankles. You knew right away I wasn't a threat. Still, you dodged your head when I tried to pet you. I don't know if there is any bite to go with your bark, but I'm glad you allowed me inside."

Tonka stretches out on the floor, rests his head on his front paws, and yawns. We've both had a long day.

"I called out to see if anyone was home, but no one answered. You poked me with your paw as though saying, 'I'm right here, dummy.' So, I bent over to try petting you again and saw the name tag on your collar. TONKA. Like the toys, right? 'Be Tonka tough!' It fits you to a T. No pun intended.

"I was still bending over when a spot of blood appeared on your white fur. I thought you had been wounded and were bleeding. Then another drop appeared next to the first one. It was like you had been hit by a tiny paintball. Only then did I realize it was me who was injured, not you!

"I reached for my temple and felt thick, warm blood seeping from a crusty wound I didn't realize I had. Applying pressure to the wound with my hand like a good Girl Scout...*am I a Scout?*...I hurried to the bathroom and found some gauze.

"I didn't look at my face in the mirror while washing my temple and applying the bandage. I can't say why. Maybe I just don't want to see my face. Maybe I have a desire to believe I'm beautiful, but fear the truth. Or maybe mean people have said hurtful things because I'm hideous and it's too painful to look. Perhaps it's because I know I'm beautiful inside and that's what truly matters. It's the echo of a truth I've been told all my life. But by who, I can't remember.

"Anyway, I stopped the bleeding and looked out the front window to learn more about where I am. Your house is on a cul-de-sac with two other homes across the street. They're dark and lifeless, too. The water was still waist deep and moving out with the force of a rip tide. Once the water recedes, I'll find out if any people are there.

"In the meantime, I began exploring your home. Not to be nosy, but to find food and something to drink and anything else I might need. You followed me to each room, making sure I behaved as a proper guest. The top level has two bedrooms, a bath and a landing that forms a loft looking down into the great room.

The lower level where the porch is has a master bedroom, bath, kitchen, pantry and great room. It's a small but nice house. Whoever lives here has taken good care of it and I'll keep it clean as long as I stay. People will return tomorrow and they can tell me who I am, right?

"Famished, I went to the refrigerator to find something to eat. I figured if the power had been out for only a few hours, the food inside would still be good. Better to eat it before it goes bad and save the food in the pantry for later, right?

"When I opened the door...surprise! The light came on. A moment later, its compressor motor kicked in. It makes so little noise it's easy to see how I had missed it. Curious, I flipped the switch for the kitchen's overhead light. Nothing. I flipped another. Still nothing.

"Your house must have an alternative power source, but provides only enough electricity for essentials like the fridge. Still starving, I decided to figure it out later and treated myself to a ham and cheese sandwich and a glass of milk. I let you have a leftover hot dog. Please, don't ever tell the dog nutrition Nazis I did that."

The Westie blinks and I swear he smiles at me. Our pact sealed, his eyelids droop, triggering a switch inside me I can't resist. I'm exhausted and my stomach is full.

"You know what?" I say, realizing I'm too tired to experiment with the power setup. "Figuring out how many appliances can run without overloading the circuit can wait until tomorrow. Right now, I have to sleep."

Unconcerned, Tonka rises long enough to walk over to his doggy bed next to the unpowered TV and lies down.

"We'll be OK until someone comes back for you," I say. "In the meantime, there's plenty to drink, plenty of food in the refrigerator, and plenty of your food in the pantry. We just need a good night's sleep. Everything will look brighter in the morning. I promise."

But the dog named after tough old toys was already asleep. I smile and count my blessings, such as they are. Retelling the day's events has given me perspective and a feeling everything truly will be OK.

I'm ready for bed, too, but I don't want to sleep in the homeowners' bed. I mean, who wants to use somebody else's funky sheets? Yuck! So, I find a blanket and lie on the couch in the great room with all the windows. It makes sense to stay on the first level in case the owners return. The wind is still howling like crazy, so there's no way I'll hear anybody coming.

I'm almost asleep when Tonka startles me, jumping onto the end of the couch where my feet rest. He blinks at me and somehow, I know he's saying, "I think you're OK, so give me some room."

I'm glad for the company.

CHAPTER TWO

Gone

Bright light from the rising sun shining through the wall of glass windows and doors wakes me early. The wind has calmed a good bit, though an occasional gust buffets the house. Chirping birds announce their relief at having survived the storm and the promise of a far better day. Tonka jumps to the floor, stretches and looks at me with expectation.

"Yeah, yeah," I say. "I know the drill. Hold your water."

But how do I know? Do I have a dog in my real life? The shock and adrenaline rush of yesterday are gone, replaced with dread and doubt. Memories from before the storm are nonexistent. I don't know who I am, where I am, or where I'm from. Why the heck was I on a sailboat during a hellacious storm? My whole life is a blank. I need answers.

The crosscurrent of emotions is overwhelming. I'm frozen with indecision, unable to decide which way to go first.

"Solve one problem at a time," the voice inside me says. "Sometimes, life comes at you fast. Decide what's most important at that moment and focus on it. The rest will fall in place."

A cold, wet nose pokes my calf, giving me my first task. It's a simple request. One that gives me direction. But I need to get my bearings before going outside, so I step out onto the back porch to survey my surroundings.

The floodwaters are gone, revealing a lot I couldn't see yesterday. The sailboat blocks the stairs...can't go that way. I also see a pier crossing over the marsh to a creek a hundred yards away. It flows east toward what must be a river. It is a beautiful setting. The water level must have been six or eight feet above normal. Any less and the sailboat wouldn't have cleared the pier.

"I can't fathom why I was out there...alone," I say to Tonka. He answers by poking me with his nose again.

I have two choices...either take the front stairs or the enclosed stairway descending from the middle of the house. The enclosed stairway doesn't allow me to see what's outside, so forget that idea.

"I'll take door number one, Wayne!"

Instead of acknowledging my timely "Let's Make a Deal" reference, Tonka positions himself in front of the door. When I open it, he hits the steps on a dead run. While he does his business, I survey the area from the elevated front porch. There are fallen trees and debris everywhere, but it's a beautiful morning. If no one comes back, at least I can explore. The weather won't be an issue. Things are looking up!

While Tonka checks out the rearranged landscape and unfamiliar smells, I create a mental list of what to do next. First...eat some breakfast. Then...find somebody. Anybody. There must be someone around here somewhere.

When Tonka is done, I go to the fridge and gather a bounty of grapes, bacon, cheese, and eggs. As I cook breakfast, I'm constantly looking out the kitchen window overlooking the driveway and cul-de-sac, expecting the owners to return. It will be awkward explaining why I've invaded their house and am stealing their food, but I have to believe they will understand. Especially when they see the sailboat.

I share half of the scrambled cheese-eggs with Tonka, which makes him a happy canine. I keep an eye on the cul-de-sac while eating, but no one walks by or drives up to the house. It makes sense, though. If the storm was a hurricane, then it's no wonder everyone left. Whatever.

Refreshed and refueled, I'm eager to know more about my surroundings. First, I grab a handful of small dog biscuits from the pantry and put them in my pocket. Then I find a leash hanging on a wall next to the brooms and mops and hook it to Tonka's collar. Time to go knocking on doors.

Tonka's house is on a single street with a cul-de-sac at each end. There's a short connector to a main road that goes to...I have no idea. There are thirteen houses on the street, nine of them built along the creek. Half the lots still have trees, though most of these aren't on the creek side of the road. I guess the waterfront sites are more in demand.

My plan is simple. Start with the closest house and work my way down the street. So, the first place I visit is next door, the house I saw yesterday from the back porch. Like Tonka's home, it's built atop pylons and seems to have survived the storm undamaged. I knock on the door, but no one answers. It's disappointing, but not surprising. I've not seen any signs of people at all.

Moving to the next house, I make a troubling discovery. Built close to the ground on a simple foundation, this home has been flooded. Its garage door was knocked off its rails by the weight of the water that built up inside. Debris carried out by the release of water is strewn across the driveway and front yard. Whoever lives here will be in for a big disappointment when they return. Their home is ruined.

Half of the houses are built close to the ground and have been flooded. There's no point knocking on those doors. If people had stayed inside, the flooding would have driven them out. So, we continue on to the elevated houses, knocking on each door. But nobody ever answers.

"Maybe they all left before the storm," I say to Tonka as I sit down on the front steps of the last house. "That makes sense if it was a hurricane. But why did the owners of your home leave you behind? How could they leave a little fella like you? That's way too heartless."

Sensing my angst, Tonka sits next to me on the step and licks my hand. Without thinking, I rub his ears, then realize we have crossed a threshold. He's trusting me more and his acceptance gives me hope we will become friends.

From where we're sitting, I can see the point where the creek runs into the river. It's a wide river! Maybe a mile across. I also see several houses on the other side and dozens of sailboats anchored in between.

"There must be a marina nearby," I say. "People knew a storm was coming because they moved their boats to open water. If left moored to the docks, the boats could have been damaged or destroyed. That's what you're supposed to do when there's a big storm."

Tonka just looks at me.

"No. I don't know how I know that. But one thing seems sure, I have some connection to sailing. And if I can get to one of those boats, I bet you I can sail it."

I file the idea away in my mental "Hold That Thought for Later" folder and continue my visual survey. To the south, through the wooded area at the end of the street, I see several more houses, most of them facing the river. There may be more houses beyond those.

My instinct is to continue, but it seems pointless. There are no signs of people anywhere. The more I see, the more I'm convinced the storm was a massive hurricane. Perhaps a Cat Four or Five. Only stupid people hunker down in their homes during a storm that big. Then another thought hits me.

"You know, Tonka, there's almost always dumb people who try riding out a hurricane. I'd bet dollars to doughnuts there are bodies in some of these houses. Maybe some floating around in the water, too."

Tonka growls like he's expecting to see dead people. I shudder.

"Hey, you don't think, maybe, *I* was one of the stupid people who tried to ride it out, do you?"

The thought kicks my imagination into overdrive. Why the heck was I in a sailboat during a hurricane? I have no way of knowing what my aptitudes and IQ are, but I don't feel like I'm a dummy. But who knows?

"No," I say, more to myself than Tonka. "I can't be that stupid. If I was on a sailboat during a hurricane, it was for good reason. Or because I had no choice. Does anybody know I'm missing? Is anybody looking for me?"

These are disturbing thoughts, ones I don't dare dwell on, given my circumstance. I push them out of my mind.

I'm champing at the bit to search the houses across the way. But if I do, I won't have time to complete my other task before dark. Knocking on those doors will have to wait until tomorrow.

As we pass the wooded lots on the way back, a raccoon staggers out of the underbrush, crossing the street in front of us. Tonka and I freeze in place, but it's too late. The raccoon sees us, rises on its hind legs and hisses. I tighten my grip on the leash. I know trashcan bandits are shy creatures, not prone to coming close to humans in the wild. The raccoon may just be surprised...or it may have rabies. If he bites either of us, it'll be bad news.

Before I can step back, Tonka bolts toward the raccoon, yanking the leash out of my hand. The creature hisses again and puffs out its fur to look bigger. The Westie comes within inches of the coon, puts on his brakes and barks for all he's worth. Intimidated, the raccoon turns tail, scrambles back to the woods and up a pine tree. Tonka nips at his heels, barely missing, then raises up to plant his front paws on the tree trunk. He stares up into the branches, daring the raccoon to come down. It is a classic coon dog treeing pose.

And how the heck do I know that?

"Come!" I call to Tonka. Satisfied the raccoon isn't coming back, the feisty white Westie comes to me, his chest puffed out, bulldog style.

"You really are Tonka Tough, aren't you?" I rub his head and give him one of the dog biscuits in my pocket.

I pick his leash up off the pavement and unclasp it from his collar. If I hadn't lost my grip, things could have ended differently. Tonka may not have been able to dodge the raccoon if he had attacked. Keeping the Westie on a leash might do more harm than good, depending on the situation. He needs to be free to run away or to defend himself. I just have to trust that if we're separated for any reason, he'll eventually come home.

Back at Tonka's house, there are a couple of things I want to do before going inside. The sailboat is still resting against the stairway, and unless someone brings a giant crane, that's where it will remain until the next flood. There's no way I can move it. Even if I could, I wouldn't be able to haul it to the creek. It's too far away. It's a good thing this house has two more stairways. This one is useless.

With that settled, I walk down the pier a few yards and turn to look at the roof. Just as I suspected! Solar panels are mounted on either side of a single dormer...the refrigerator's power source.

I'm also able to see the name of the sailboat painted in big black letters near the stern. CHALLENGER. Dozens of random thoughts flash through my mind.

Memories of astronaut Judy Resnik, the teacher Christa McAuliffe, and the terrible explosion that killed them and the rest of the crew play in my head like a video. But nothing about the sailboat or me bubbles up from my memory. *Why am I able to recall things about astronauts and space shuttles, but nothing about who I am or why I was on a stupid sailboat? This has to be the lamest amnesia in history.*

Pushing my aggravation aside, Tonka and I go back inside the house to the top floor and locate a pull-down ladder to the attic. The springs make loud twanging noises when I unfold the ladder and I wonder how safe the thing is. The steps creak as I go up, but hold OK. When I'm high enough, I stop and look around. Sure enough, at one end of the attic is a bank of batteries to store energy from the solar cells. Now, to find the last piece of this alternative energy puzzle.

Downstairs in the pantry area, I locate two electrical panels...one to handle the main power coming from the street and one to handle power from the batteries. And...hot darn...there are instructions on laminated paper explaining how to switch from one to the other. There's also a list showing which combination of electrical items can be used at the same time without tripping the breaker. Easy peasy, lemon squeezy!

Wait! Did I really just say easy peasy and hot darn? Am I a nerd? OMG, please don't tell me I'm a nerd!

Whatever.

Cowplop! I did it again. Only dorks say whatever. At least I say cowplop. Saying cowplop is a bad girl thing, right?

OK, enough of this nonsense. I yam what I yam, as Popeye used to say. I've got more pressing issues to deal with, as Tonka now reminds me. He's poking me with his nose again, telling me it's time to eat.

It's been a long day, and it's almost dark. After figuring out which electrical switches to flip, I direct power to a lamp in the main room and turn on the ceiling fan. The refrigerator stays on no matter what. That it still works is the biggest blessing I have received in this great big pile of bad fortune.

I feed Tonka and eat something too, though I'm not hungry. I'm so tired I'm just stuffing random food from the fridge in my mouth. It's been a day and a half since crawling out of the sailboat and still no signs of other people. Nothing. My thoughts turn back to where they started this morning. If I'm missing, shouldn't someone be looking for me? It was a big storm. Maybe a hurricane. So, where are the search and rescue teams? Where are the people returning to their homes? Shouldn't there be firemen and police?

"Is this house on an island?" I ask Tonka. "Or maybe we're on a peninsula and the roads are blocked?"

Tired, I turn off the light and lie on the couch, hoping that sleep will come quickly. Tonka jumps up to take his spot at the end. The only noise is the soft hum of the fan overhead.

Just as I'm about to slip into the blissful unawareness of sleep, a chilling thought pops into my mind. In one swift movement, I whip off the blanket, dash to the back porch, and open the screen door. Standing above Challenger, I look up at the sky.

Another chill hits me like the bucket of ice water poured on me as part of a fundraising challenge. *Another recovered memory to be explored later.* There is nothing to see but stars. With no ambient light to dim their brilliance, I see billions and billions of stars shining in the night sky. The sky is crystal clear and the stars are dazzling. I can see the Milky Way in all its glory on the southeast horizon.

But it isn't what I see that scares me, it's what I don't see. There's not one flashing light to be seen moving across the sky. Where are the airplanes?

CHAPTER THREE

Alone

Once again, the morning sun shining through the windows and glass doors wakes me. My sleep was sporadic. I'm stiff and not well-rested. The mystery of the missing airplanes tumbled through my mind all night. And still no signs of people.

There're at least a dozen reasons rescue and recovery aircraft might not be flying around. It's a lot harder to explain why there were no lights from commercial airliners or military planes at the higher altitudes. Maybe it was a quirk of schedules, flight paths, or atmospheric conditions. But now it's daylight, and I will either confirm or refute my theory.

"Here goes nothing," I say to Tonka as I head toward the back porch. Like last night, I walk out to the back steps and look upward.

The air is clear. The temperature is cool, hinting of fall weather. The sky is...empty. No contrails. No light glinting off the metal skins of aircraft. No distant roar of jet turbines or gas engines. Nothing.

I step back onto the porch and sit on a lounger before my knees buckle. Tonka jumps up beside me, poking his nose under my forearm so my hand rests on his head.

"This is bad, Tonka. Real bad. I don't know where I am, but I know I should be seeing airliners. You'd have to be in the middle of nowhere...some remote place on the planet...to not see any planes jetting through upper altitudes."

A hot surge of panic threatens to throw me off-kilter. I struggle to keep my cool.

"Focus," the voice inside my head says. "One step at a time. Accomplish one thing, then move on to the next."

All the things I had done yesterday whirl through my mind in a blur. They had all needed to be done. I did them all well. What's the most important thing I need to do right now? Then it hits me.

"How stupid can I be?" I say, slapping my forehead. Yeah, I actually slapped my forehead like some kind of dork. On top of everything else, I'm concerned about my nerd tendencies.

Like a whirlwind, I return to the great room, searching for something that tells where I am. Mail. Maybe some magazines with address stickers. A checkbook. Anything!

It hadn't occurred to me to look yesterday because I was just gonna ask the first person I saw. But nobody showed up. And now I'm not sure they're going to.

Nothing! There's not a single magazine or old envelope anywhere. Incredible!

OK. This is nuts. Either the people who live here are the biggest clean freaks on the planet or I must be living in an episode of Stranger Things. Or a bad Kendare Blake novel...not that she has any.

Aaannddd...how do I know about Stranger Things and Kendare Blake? Are they things I like? Or did I make fun of them? The needle on my personal Dork Meter is pegging out on the "I Like Them" side of the scale. Lord help me.

As I file the pop culture references in my "Hold That Thought for Later" folder, I spot a drawer underneath the countertop peninsula separating the great room from the kitchen. I look inside.

Boom! Oh yeah! Not only do I find a stack of bills, there're also several takeout menus and a map. I take out the map and discover I *might* be in a place named New Bern, North Carolina.

It sounds familiar, but it could be because of the state's name. I mean, I know all the state's names. Who doesn't? But the name New Bern doesn't reboot my scrambled memory bank. So now the question is, does the map correlate to where I am? Or did Tonka's people pick up the map while on a visit?

I grab a bill from the top of the stack and there it is…23 Shadow Lane, New Bern, NC. The next bill says the same. They all say, Shadow Lane.

Yes!

Looking at one of the takeout menus, I see it's for a pizza restaurant named Big Susie's on Broad Creek Road and…BINGO! Its location appears on a small inset on the back panel. Though the restaurant isn't in New Bern, the map shows the town is close, just on the other side of a river.

I open the "Map of New Bern" and figure out where Susie's is located. Shadow Lane must be somewhere close by. The longer I look, the more frustrated I am. If I had a working laptop or a smartphone, I could find it in two nano seconds. But the street *has* to be on this map somewhere, so I keep looking, methodically moving my finger over each road connecting to Broad Creek. Compared to a town or city, there aren't many, but it seems to take forever. After about ten or fifteen minutes…there it is!

Just my luck. Of course, Shadow Lane is at the end of Broad Creek Road, or else I would have found it sooner. Whatever. At least I know where I am, even if I don't know anything about it. From the map, I can see that Broad Creek Road stops at a body of water named…you guessed it…Broad Creek. I also see that Broad Creek flows into the Neuse River. The house and the entire area are on a fat peninsula.

"So...Tonka. I know where I am. What do I do now?"

He looks in the direction where the dog food is kept, and I realize the morning is flying by. We both need breakfast.

My mind is racing. Half of me believes I've fallen into some insane alignment of coincidences and the other half...and growing stronger by the minute...believes that something horrific has happened. I need to figure out which it is. I'm done with waiting for people to show up!

I'm still cramming dry cereal in my mouth as Tonka and I leave the house. To carry supplies, I've stuffed a small backpack I found with two apples, a box of raisins, a single pack of saltine crackers, a brick of cheddar cheese, and a jar of peanut butter. There's also a large zip-lock plastic bag filled with dog food and a smaller one containing dog treats. A bota bag filled with water is strapped under the pack's outside flap and there's a small flashlight in a side pocket. The map I found is tucked into the front of my pants where I can grab it without having to remove the backpack. Strapped to my belt is a hunting knife. In my hands, I carry a crowbar that was in a storage room beneath the house...just in case. It has a nice heft to it.

My plan is to explore as much of the area before dark as possible. It seems unlikely another whole day will pass without finding somebody, but I've brought enough food to last me a couple of days if need be.

There's an unspoken truth bouncing around in my head that goes, "If you return to Tonka's home without finding anybody, you've got bigger problems than you can imagine." So, the mind game I'm playing is that I won't go back. I'll keep looking until I find somebody. Anybody. Somebody has to be here, somewhere.

"OK," I say to Tonka as we approach the house next door. "I'm not playing around anymore. Let's find out where everybody went."

To be on the safe side, I knock on the door to make sure no one came home when I wasn't looking. Nothing. Next, I pound on the door with the crowbar. Still nothing. I shove the end of the crowbar into the doorjamb and pull. The wood creaks but doesn't give. As far as I know, I've never done anything like this. It can't be but so hard.

I try again. The wood still doesn't give. Frustrated, I repeatedly jab the crowbar's sharp tip into the door frame until the wood around the deadbolt splinters away. I pry on the door again and...it swings open!

Tonka jumps inside ahead of me, exploring each room to make sure it's safe to enter. Despite my earlier bravado, I now worry that breaking into someone's house is a big mistake.

"Let's make this quick, Tonka. It would be just my luck the people who live here will drive up while we're inside. Which begs the question, what *is* my luck factor? It's so weird not having memories. I might be one of the luckiest people in the world. But then again, if I was lucky, I wouldn't be in this situation. Or would I? That question can't be answered until I find out what happened to everybody else."

Still concerned about being caught in the act, I dash through each room, checking for anything that can tell me where the people went. Maybe a note on the countertop or a message taped on the refrigerator. Anything.

But there's nothing.

As I head back to the front door, my shoe slips on the hardwood floor and I almost do the splits. One thing is for sure, there's no way I'm a gymnast. That hurt!

Kneeling for a closer look, I discover the cause of my near accident is a random pile of sand and glass. I poke at it with my finger and uncover a gold wedding band and a metal belt buckle.

"This is weird," I say to Tonka, rubbing the slippery aggregate between my fingers. "It feels like silica." *Silica? Where the heck did that word come from?* "The house is spotless except for this one pile of sand. It must have spilled from a container or something as the people were leaving."

The Westie sniffs at the pile but isn't impressed. He can't eat it, so...not interested.

"Oh...my...god! You don't think that maybe this is a pile of ash that spilled from an urn, do you? That might explain the ring and buckle, but... No. That doesn't seem right. It's gotta be something else."

I pack the thought away as yet another mystery to solve and head to the next house. With a little less trouble than before...I pry the door open. Again, no signs of people or where they went. On to the next house.

By lunch time, we've broken into every home on the street that hadn't flooded and find nothing to help solve the mystery of their disappearance, except...

It's not an answer. Not really. It's its own mystery. About half the houses have small piles of sand like the one in the first house. Sometimes there are two or three. Most of them contain rings or small diamonds or other such artifact. There's no pattern as to which rooms they're in. The locations are random. It's like a demented Sand Man visited certain houses, dropping random scoops of sand and salt wherever the mood struck him. Strange.

I'm getting hungry, so we stop to sit on the steps of the same house we paused at yesterday. The apple is tart, just the way I like it. *Another note about who I am for the file.* I give Tonka a dog biscuit and we share some water. Dark clouds are forming off in the distance. It looks like we may have an afternoon storm.

"I should've looked for a raincoat, Tonka. I'll check the coat closets in the next houses to see if I can find one. Hey! Wouldn't it be cool if we find one that fits you?"

It was supposed to be funny, but I realize I have to do a better job thinking things through. I'm not in this alone. If Tonka is to be my faithful companion, I need to consider his safety as much as mine.

"Faithful companion," I repeat out loud. "Should I start calling you Tonto instead of Tonka?"

I have no idea how I know Tonto was the Lone Ranger's faithful Indian companion. Do I watch a lot of old TV shows?

My nerd alert is ringing again. Time to move on.

We're in unfamiliar territory now, at least unfamiliar to me. We break into some of the houses on the waterfront I had seen yesterday. Most of them were flooded during the storm, so we skip those. Spending energy to open doors swollen shut by the water and trudging through wet carpeted floors just isn't worth it. We focus on the places that are still habitable.

By this time, my door-opening skills are bona fide. I can break into a house in a matter of seconds. I've learned that using the crooked end of the bar and throwing my shoulder into it will open almost any door on the first try. I've also learned how easy it is to open patio glass doors. It's stupid easy. People would be shocked to learn that, with a crowbar, you can lift the entire sliding door out of its track and pull the thing out in two seconds. So much for security.

There's another thing we've discovered. Something disturbing. Some homes have pets trapped inside. That's why we always knock first. If a dog barks...big or small...we leave the house alone. I can't take a chance on Tonka or me being attacked. It might seem cruel, but it's still possible people will return. I'd feel terrible if someone came home to find their fur babies missing. *Fur babies?! I say fur babies? Gag.* Not just missing, but released by a misguided stranger. Leaving them where they are seems the better course of action for all concerned. At least for now.

Cats are a different matter. They don't always make their presence known when I knock. I mean, they're cats, right? Most times, we can't tell if there's a cat even after we're inside, unless they come out of hiding. To his credit, and my relief, Tonka doesn't attack them. He just stares at them like they are alien creatures. Whenever I see signs of cats, I take the time to fill their food and water bowls before leaving.

By midafternoon, we're done exploring the entire area, so I study the map to decide where to go next. It's a no-brainer. Like I said, I'm on a peninsula and I've explored everything on the tip. The next neighborhood is on the other side of the main road. The streets loop around small lakes, and after a few blocks, connect to a marina.

As we travel deeper into the subdivision, the community's outward appearance changes. There are fewer houses and more patio homes and condos. The condos appear to be vacation rental units. I can tell they are rentals because the people occupying them are living out of suitcases. Also, there are no family pictures on the walls, and they all have "Things to Do in New Bern" brochures lying around. By evening, we have entered twice as many homes and houses as we did this morning. I'm exhausted, but there's one more place I want to go before nightfall.

On the way, we walk by dozens of homes and rental units we've yet to break into. And still no sign of human life. No cars or trucks moving on the roads. No planes in the air. No boaters on the water. I force myself not to dwell on what that means. I know it's bad. I'm just not ready to consider how bad.

The marina is different from what I expected. Between the road and the docks is a large, two-story building with no signage declaring its purpose. Between the road and the building...strangely out of place in this vacation-land setting...stands a massive cell phone tower. One of those giant mast-like structures with several antennas at the top.

"I bet folks around here have excellent cell phone service," I say to Tonka. My attempt at being snarky brings new questions bubbling into my consciousness. Do I own a cell phone? If so, where is it? What happened to it? Is it on the sailboat?

I never went back inside the boat because I had no need to. I was sure I'd soon be with other people, and they would answer my questions. Now, I realize, I need to take a closer look at the vessel that brought me to this strange land.

From the street, Tonka and I are looking at the back of the two-story building. The front faces the water instead of the road. Occupying the space between the building and the marina, we see a large, empty patio. Empty except for a huge mound of tables and chairs, piled in one corner, deposited by the receding floodwaters.

"It's a restaurant," I say to Tonka. "And look, it has guest rooms on the second level. Pity. There's so much damage, it'll be a long time before anybody eats here again."

As I scan the marina, I'm surprised to see half the boats are still afloat. Dozens are resting akimbo on the piers. Several are perched atop other boats, creating random death traps. Some are underwater, their bow and stern lines still tied to dock cleats as though refusing to accept their altered state. Yet, many of the boats aren't damaged at all and appear seaworthy.

It's not a huge marina, perhaps a hundred slips. The cove it's in must be manmade, though it's hard to tell. It's protected on three sides by land, its fourth side opening into a stream to the river. The stream's far side is bordered by a spit of undeveloped land, its trees providing a barrier against the open water and the wind. The marina is well-situated to stand up to the brunt of a hurricane and explains why so many of the vessels survived.

As Tonka and I navigate the boats, storage boxes and other debris cluttering the piers and docks, the unease that's gripped my chest all day grows tighter. I don't know why. Perhaps it's the eerie quiet. Where normally there would be dozens of people engaged in conversations, making repairs, recovering boats, and coming together to help each other...there is only silence.

The air is so still there aren't any ripples lapping against the pylons and boat hulls. If it wasn't for the occasional call of a gull and the sound of our footsteps, I would wonder if I had lost my hearing. And if not for Tonka's companionship, I'm sure my calm demeanor would evaporate in two seconds.

We reach the end of the main pier where the boats refuel. I unsling my backpack, remove the bag of dog treats and sit on the edge of the dock, legs dangling over the water. Tonka sits beside me. We're facing due west and the sun is about to drop behind the trees across the creek.

"I don't know, Tonka," I say, giving him a treat. "I don't know where everyone is, and I don't have a clue what we should do next. I was sure we would find someone, or someone would find us. It's been two and a half days. I... I..."

A knot forms in my throat so big it hurts. My eyes water, but I clench my jaw so hard I hear my teeth gritting. I...WILL...NOT...CRY.

"We're going to be OK," I say in a whisper, pulling Tonka closer. "You and me, little buddy. We're going to be OK. I promise."

CHAPTER FOUR

Que Será

I wake, stiff and cold. Tonka is nestled against my stomach, sharing body warmth. The backpack supports my head. It makes a lousy pillow. I hadn't meant to fall asleep on the dock, but that's where I find myself. Lying on the rough planks with no cushion or cover. I shiver. Tonka stirs.

"The weather is changing," I say, gazing at the dark clouds that moved in overnight. "Well, it is October. We don't have to worry about freezing cold temperatures yet, but we need to prepare. That is, if we don't find anybody."

A bolt of lightning splits the sky, striking the cell tower just beyond the dock-side building. Before my brain grasps the danger, the thunder that follows reverberates through my body and sucks the air from my lungs. I almost wet my pants. Then the clouds let loose, dumping an ocean of rain on our heads. The entire event has taken less than two seconds, but I can see Tonka is already at the building, taking shelter in the entryway.

I wind my way back around the debris to join Tonka under the portico. A tug on the door tells me it's locked, so out comes my trusty crowbar. One hard yank and it opens like a kid's present on Christmas morning. Easy peasy, lemon squeezy. *I have GOT to stop saying that!*

There's little ambient light coming through the windows, and it takes a moment for my eyes to adjust. The first thing I see is a bar with no barstools. Beyond the bar area is an empty dining room, its tables and chairs nowhere in sight.

"This place was closed long before the hurricane," I say to Tonka. "It's doubtful I'll find anything of use, but at least we have shelter from the storm."

I poke around a little to make sure everything is copesetic while Tonka curls up on a rug. Picking up an old menu at the hostess desk, I skim over the dishes they once served. BIG mistake. A picture of a juicy cheeseburger with a side order of fries looks so good my mouth waters.

So, what if I'm a vegetarian or a vegan? I already know I love animals. I could be a vegetarian. If I am...and that was a real cheeseburger...I would be totally blowing that diet choice.

Enough of that. I put the menu down and begin poking around the cabinets and closets. Nada. It's completely dark in the kitchen because there aren't any windows. So I retrieve the flashlight from the backpack before heading in.

The place has been gutted. Instead of an oven and a dishwasher, there are empty spaces. There's no grill either. No plates. No glasses. No pots or pans. Nothing.

But as I turn to leave, my flashlight beam falls on a utility cart in the corner, the kind housekeeping uses. And it's loaded with clean, folded-up, red tablecloths. Score!

I grab an armful, go back to Tonka and give him a quick rubdown to dry him off. When I'm done, he shakes himself, then gives me a playful headbutt. He thinks it's a game, but this isn't the time. I throw a dry tablecloth on the mat, and he curls up on it, snug and dry.

With Tonka taken care of, I undress, dry off, and wrap a dry tablecloth around me to keep warm. I spread my wet clothes out on the floor to dry.

Now what? It's still raining, and it will be awhile before my clothes dry. I've got nothing to do. Time to collect my thoughts and put a plan together. I see a manager's office beyond the bar, so I grab the flashlight and take my red toga-clad-self inside to find a pen and something to write on.

Even better than loose-leaf paper, I discover a stack of unused accounting ledgers. I pick one up and see that their pages are printed with well-defined lines and sections. And now I'm feeling really stupid.

The orderly pages force me to realize how *un*organized my approach to exploring has been. I should be keeping a list of everything I've seen in the houses. The things that might be useful later. Not to mention listing addresses of places where pets are trapped inside. If the owners don't return, it will be up to me to let their pets out. Listing their locations will save time later.

And there it is. The big fat truth I've been avoiding can no longer be denied. Whatever forced people to leave, they were so afraid of it they abandoned their pets. People don't do that because of hurricanes. There's plenty of warning before a storm to pack up the pets, too. And if the threat was so imminent people abandoned their pets, that threat might be ongoing. I could be in real danger...right now!

Maybe there's a nuclear power plant nearby ready to go into meltdown. Maybe it already did and I'm walking around in radioactive fallout. Maybe there was a biological outbreak that makes only humans sick. That would explain why the animals are here, but the people aren't. Maybe war was declared and I'm sitting at soon-to-be-ground zero?

"OK, Ivy Moon. Get a grip. It can't be anything that bad. And even if it is, there's nothing you can do about it. So put your big girl panties on and take care of the right-here-and-now."

I cast a glance at Tonka, who's still hunkered down on the tablecloth. I hope he didn't hear me just say "big girl panties." He peers back at me, his head resting on outstretched legs. I swear he looks annoyed.

Speaking my name calms me down. And somehow, I know the "big girl" comment and the que será attitude come from my past. Someone used to say that kind of stuff to me. If *only* I could remember who!

"It's time we head back to the house," I say to Tonka as I pull on my still-damp clothes. "I need to regroup. I need to figure out what's happened. And I need a plan"

CHAPTER FIVE

Best Laid Plans

Tonka is perched atop an ottoman in front of the freestanding woodstove, staring at the flames behind its thick glass doors. It is, as I've discovered, super-efficient. The intake vent is almost closed, yet the stove burns so hot I'm forced to open a door to the porch now and then to cool off. Tonka, however, can't seem to get enough. I half fear that if I open the woodstove's door to throw in another log, he might jump in.

"Hey, little buddy," I say, "why don't you back off a little? Take a break. It's not that cold, yet."

He continues to stare through the glass into the fire. Whatever. He'll move when he gets too hot.

The front that brought the rain was a cold one. The summer-like weather we had enjoyed was chased away by fall's chill. Our return trip to Tonka's cottage was wet and miserable, drawn out by numerous stops at houses we had already visited. I entered the address of each home in my logbook along with the items that might be of future use. The garages are like gold mines for someone in need of survival gear. Equipment like axes, garden wagons, chainsaws, tillers, and even golf carts made my list. The plans fermenting in my brain require the use of all those things.

Of course, the ledger also lists the locations of pantries stocked with non-perishable food items. That nobody is coming to my rescue is almost a certainty. I have to think long term now. Not just in terms of food, but clothing as well.

In that regard, my ledger has only one crummy address listed. It's one of the rental units, and it's only one suitcase. Judging by the places I've broken into so far, nobody my size and age lives around here. According to the map, we have hundreds of houses and units yet to explore. I hope we'll have better luck with those, but at least I scored two pairs of jeans, three shirts and some underwear.

The ledger also notes...in bold red ink...all the places with animals trapped inside. I can't adopt them or take care of them. I know that. But I won't leave them inside to die of starvation or thirst. Some situations will be risky, but I can't help that. I have to do it. I'll hate myself if I don't.

After starting a fire, I had spread the ledger and map out on the coffee table by the woodstove. My map is now flagged with places to return to and fresh places to explore. I've made so many notes, my fingers are cramping. But I'm warm, dry, well-fed, and safe. This place I'm in...Tonka's home...is truly a blessing. I mean, I even have lamp light to write by while the rest of the world around me sits in total darkness. All things considered...I can't imagine having ended up in a better situation.

"I think it's time to call it a night," I say to Tonka as I fold up the map. "How about a bedtime snack?

The milk in the fridge is still good, so I pour a glass, grab a couple of oatmeal-raisin cookies, and sit on the couch next to Tonka's perch. I munch on a cookie and join the Westie in fire gazing. The scent of burning oak permeates the room, providing some much-appreciated aroma therapy to soothe my psyche.

Aroma therapy? What do I know about aroma therapy?

A thousand thoughts, theories, and fears swirl through my head. And just to add bitter icing to a foul cake, loneliness infects my mood.

"There will be none of that!" I say, attempting to stave off negative vibes.

Tonka looks at me and spots the cookie I haven't eaten yet. And just like that, he's not interested in the fire anymore.

"Ok," I say, breaking the cookie apart. "I'll let you have some of the oatmeal part, but *no* raisins. Raisins are toxic to dogs."

Now, how do I know that?

More than a nuisance, the mystery of who I am is driving me nuts. It's like a splendid dream you can't remember the next morning. It's bad enough that there's no one to talk to. Not being able to converse with my past self makes it worse. As far as self-awareness, I'm only four-days old. I don't know anybody or anything.

"Enough of this pity party," I sigh.

I wash the cookie crumbs down with the rest of the milk and wrap the blanket around me.

"Tomorrow, I'm going into the sailboat to see if I can find clues as to who I am," I say to Tonka, who's reclaimed his spot on the ottoman. "You can watch from the porch. Maybe something inside will tell me who I am."

CHAPTER SIX

The Boat

Tonka peers at me through the porch screen as I descend the steps and climb aboard Challenger. The vessel remains tilted toward the house, leaning against the stairs where it came to rest. Traversing the deck is tricky given the severe slant, but I make it to the hatch OK.

Though I don't remember having closed it, I'm glad to see that it is. Everything inside should be nice and dry. I mean, who wants to climb around inside a soggy boat cabin?

I slide the hatch open. Musty air infused with smells of motor oil, cooking odors, diesel, and teakwood awaken suppressed sensory perceptions. Familiar, yet vague. Memories of nautical terms and experiences force their way into my consciousness, like silhouettes just beyond the reach of a streetlamp. I try to will them into the full light, but it's just not happening.

Steeling my resolve, I take a deep breath and descend the steps into the cabin's interior. It takes a minute for my eyes to adjust to the dim light and I see...nothing. Nothing unusual. It's just an ordinary sailboat cabin.

From where I'm standing, portside is on the left, starboard on the right. To the left of the stairway is a sink. A countertop housing the stovetop and microwave wraps around toward the stern. To the right is a tiny bathroom...or head...as it's called in nautical terms.

How the heck do I know this stuff?

Farther inside, amidships, I see a dinette with seats on either side. It's one of those setups where the table can be removed and turned into a sleeping berth. On the left is the berth I was in when I rolled onto the deck. There aren't any sheets or covers, so I hadn't been using it as a bed. Had I passed out? Fainted? Did someone put me there? Another mystery.

At eye level, running along each side of the cabin, are two series of rectangular portholes covered with small curtains. I slide the curtain back on the closest porthole and light floods the living area.

A combination chart table-communication station is tucked into the space between the dinette and the head. Over the table, attached to a pivoting arm that allows it to be stowed away, is a small computer. Secured within the bulkhead next to the station is a bank of radios and navigation electronics.

At last...I spot what I'd hope to find. Except, there's nothing there. I mean, there's an electrical panel with charging cables, but no cell phones. My heart sinks. I know I have a smartphone. I don't know how. But I feel it in my DNA. Every girl in the civilized world has a smartphone, right? Vague images of social media wastelands, texting and surfing the Internet pique my memory. If I own a phone...and I'm sure I do...it has to be here somewhere!

Sailboats like these are chock full of compartments and hidden storage nooks. So, I start opening drawers and cupboards at a furious pace. When I run out of storage areas to check, I drop to the deck, thinking it may have fallen on the floor. Nothing.

I spy the captain's quarters at the bow and search there as well. Then the guest quarters at the stern. And the small closet next to it. I find a couple of pairs of jeans and several blouses. Are they mine? Who knows? I search every square inch of the boat's interior until I am convinced that there's nowhere else to look.

Tired and frustrated, I sit on the chair at the communication desk and stare at the dark computer screen and unlit radios. I turn each power switch to ON, hoping against hope that one of the devices work. No joy. The power was left on for days. Now the batteries are dead. Fate is conspiring against me, doing all it can to keep me from finding other people and who I am.

You're missing something, the voice in my head taunts. *You're looking right at it, but you don't see it.*

Again I look about the cabin, focusing on every detail. On the bulkhead above the radios is a corkboard. Various notes, business cards, and brochures are tacked on the board, but there's nothing specific to me. Nothing that says who I am.

Then I see it! On the corkboard are several empty spaces. Rectangular shaped open spots where the cork is darker than the surrounding area. Places where pictures had once been, blocking the light so the cork under the picture isn't faded, but the cork around the picture is. My subconscious spotted the difference, then the voice steered me toward it.

Someone had removed pictures from the board. Was it before or after the boat ran aground? Perhaps more important, were they pictures of me? If so, why had they been removed? And by whom?

Goosebumps erupt on every inch of my flesh. My senses are on fire. Everything I see, hear, taste, and smell could be a clue. I've turned into a corporeal sponge, soaking up every element of my surroundings at once. Then, like a laser, my eyes focus on a stack of blue ledgers on a shelf above the radios. I know what they are before picking one up. They are ship's logs, records of times and places where the boat has been.

I open the logbook and the pages are blank. There are no entries. It hasn't been used yet. I thumb through the other ledgers and see that they're all blank. So, where are the used logs? Every captain keeps a log. The idea the captain of this boat had logbooks but didn't use them makes no sense. There aren't any completed or current logbooks onboard. I know, because I just finished searching the entire boat. I would have noticed the bright blue cover. All completed logs and the current one had been removed. But by who, and when?

Another thought hits me. I turn back to the closet next to the guest quarters. Removing each item one at a time, I inspect the labels and dig through the pockets. As my fingers slide into the back pocket of the last pair of jeans, I feel stiff plastic. A driver's license, maybe?

The rush of finding a possible clue is squashed when I hold the card up to the light. It's a business card. A very fancy business card, for sure. But just a business card. It's made of thin, flexible metal of a type I don't recognize. A quarter of the card, at the end, looks like a screen mesh. Other than to look artsy, the design makes no sense.

Images appear on both sides. One has the engraving of a space shuttle...except it's not the shuttle. It's some kind of craft that looks similar to the shuttle. The other side is engraved with the image of an astronaut floating in space. The spacewalker has an arm raised, waving hello.

My heart skips a beat! At the bottom edge of the card is a person's name, almost impossible to see unless held at a certain angle. Typed in a font that somehow looks both ancient and futuristic is the name...Alex Steele. There's no other information. No phone number, URL, addy, or street address. I flip the card over and turn it to the correct angle. There's one word...Genesis.

For a moment, I wonder if Alex Steele is my name, but I'm not feeling a connection. I could be wrong. Who knows? While I seem able to remember almost everything I would have learned in school, I can't remember anything about who I am.

And the Genesis thing...I know the Biblical reference. But in terms of space and somebody named Alex, it doesn't mean squat to me. Did somebody give it to me and I stuck it in my back pocket? Heck, I don't even know if the clothes in the closet belong to me. They're the right size, but that doesn't prove they're mine. I've found nothing to explain how or why I was on the boat.

Frustrated, I toss the card on the table, stuff the clothes in a laundry bag, and go topside. Making sure the hatch is closed, I toss the bag to the top of the steps and climb to the porch.

Tonka, who looks like he hasn't moved from the spot I left him, greats me with a turn of his head, giving me a look that says, "I told you so." To say it tweaks me off is an understatement. I don't know why, it just does. Maybe it's because I've come to believe that, if he could talk, he could tell me things I need to know. But that's just frustration playing with my head, right? Whatever.

Exploring the boat turned out to be a big fat nothing burger, but it's the first thing on my plan, and now it's done. I know what comes next, and I'm ready. It will be hard, but at least it will keep me moving and my mind busy. Ivy Moon is ready to rock and roll!

Jeeezzz...I need some new catch lines. Something from this millennium would be good.

CHAPTER SEVEN

Next Best Thing

It's still mid-morning and I have lots to do. First, I check my list of resources and find the address where a gas-powered golf cart is located. This house and those around it were built at a higher elevation than Tonka's neighborhood. Although the garage had flooded, the water hadn't reached the cart's engine, so it should still run.

It only takes half an hour to find the house and go inside. The key is in the ignition so I give it a turn and...score! It starts right up. No problemo, as the Terminator would say. The gas gauge shows the tank is almost full. Great, but...duh. Only now do I realize the garage door is closed and there's no electricity to open it.

Cutting off the engine so as not to asphyxiate us with carbon monoxide, I study the problem for a minute. I could start the cart again and try ramming through the door? No, that won't work. The headlights or front tires could be damaged. Or the cart's canopy might collapse under the weight of the falling door. I know little about garage doors, but...

Wait, now I'm remembering what things I DON'T know? This memory loss thing is weird sometimes.

Anyway, even though I don't know how such things work, I see a handle on the door's lower panel. I'm thinking it's for raising it by hand. Yep, I'm a genius alright.

I pull on the handle but...no joy. The door doesn't budge. This sucks. I need the golf cart to carry supplies and to save time. To have a perfectly good cart with three-quarters of a tank of gas and no way to use it...not acceptable! I'm going to open this door if I have to use a can opener.

And this is the moment I realize something cool about myself. Two things, to be accurate. One, I don't quit. Not when I'm convinced the problem has a solution. And two, I have an analytical mind. I'm not sure why I think that's so cool, but I do. It's totally geeky...and I'm OK with that.

I trace the chains, cables, and rollers that make the door work and see a red cord. The cord is hanging from the middle runner and has a pull handle. I don't have to be a brainiac to understand red means something important. Like maybe an emergency release?

In terms of height, I'm pretty sure I'm average for my age...even though I'm not sure what either of those is. Anyway, the cord is too high for me to grab even when I stand on tiptoes. I could look for a ladder or a box to stand on, but I'm in a hurry.

Channeling my inner Kelsey Plum, I jump for the cord, grab the handle, and land softly on the concrete floor...with the broken red cord and handle still grasped in my hand. As Scooby-Doo would say...ruh roh. *I have GOT to stop these lame pop culture references!* Now the question is, did the lock release or did I break it?

Taking a deep breath, I squat, grasp the garage door handle, and use my legs to pull up with all the power I can muster. The door shoots up like a bottle rocket and slams to a stop in the full-open position. One side of the door jumps its track and crashes on top of the golf cart. From the corner of my eye, I see a white streak dart outside to safety as shattered glass rains down. Terrified, I cover my head with my arms in case the blasted thing falls on me.

When the tinkling of glass stops, I look up to survey the damage. The cart's canopy is dented, but still intact. The windshield, however, is a total loss. I may have an analytical mind...but I better start thinking things through before I hurt myself. Whatever. At least the door is open.

Now, how do I get the cart out?

A stepladder leaning against the wall gives me an idea. I open the legs, lock them open, and push the door up clear of the canopy. I leave the ladder under the door so it can't fall the rest of the way. Once the cart is out on the driveway, I sweep the broken glass from the cab and remove the windshield's frame.

Ready to go at last! Or maybe not. I pat the seat for Tonka to jump in, but he balks. I don't want to force him or pick him up. He needs to be comfortable with the cart. So, exercising a little patience and tempting him with a handful of dog biscuits, I coax him up onto the front seat. Our little outing involved a lot more adventure than I had expected, but we've scored a new ride and it's time to head home.

By noon, we've loaded the cart with food, water and various tools that might come in handy. The sky is clouding up again. Another cold front is about to pass through, I'm sure of it. But I have an ace in the hole. *A poker reference? Really?* Tonka's people were campers, so I also have a sleeping bag and other equipment like a propane stove, a mess kit and a gas lantern. I have no idea how long this excursion will last, but I'm prepared.

I also found a box of laminate sheeting and a clipboard in a file cabinet next to their computer. So, with my trusty resource list protected in plastic and secured on the clipboard, Tonka and I head out on our first major quest.

It's a good thing that we're doing, but still heartbreaking. Stopping at each house and condo that has a pet, we reopen the door to set them free. It hurts my heart because what I really want to do is adopt them. All of them. But that's not possible. So, I'm doing the next best thing by letting them go. At least now they can forage on their own.

It hurts because I know most of them won't make it. These are people's pets. They know nothing about fending for themselves. They know nothing about hunting, fighting, or even hiding. They're the victims of their domestication, at no fault of their own.

"Some of the cats will make it," I tell Tonka as two tabbies we release dash away. "Maybe even most of them. Well, at least the ones that still have claws and are young enough to hunt."

From his perch on the golf cart's passenger seat, Tonka's eyes follow the cats as they disappear between the houses. I know it's crazy, but I swear I see sadness in his eyes, like he understands. Somehow, I know he does.

And so it goes. The rest of the day becomes an emotional roller coaster, reveling in the knowledge we are giving these beloved pets a chance, then falling into a funk knowing their chances are slim. I'm sucker punching myself with false hope.

"I'm sorry," I say to a beautiful male malamute we free from a condo. His upper lip curls and growls when he sees Tonka. But his need to find food and water overrides his wariness of the Westie and he ambles away, perhaps in search of his people.

"He might make it," I say to Tonka as I slide into the driver's seat. "He looks pretty healthy and big enough to scare most other dogs away."

My little buddy doesn't respond, choosing instead to keep his eyes on the malamute, making sure he doesn't double back. But having said the words out loud, I realize how hollow they sound.

It's been almost a week since the storm and The Great Vanishing...the name I've given the absence of people. The trapped pets only had the food and water left in their bowls during that time. Some we've released already look weak, placing them at an even greater disadvantage.

I grip the steering wheel, but my foot refuses to push the gas pedal. Tears cascade down my cheeks and I bow my head, overwhelmed by the tragedy of it all. The longer we do this, the more the reality of what will befall these beautiful creatures outweighs our good intentions. The emotional drain is becoming too much to bear.

Sensing my pain, Tonka places his paw on my thigh. Struggling to hold back a full-blown blubber fest, I rub his head and will myself to get a grip.

"I'll be OK," I say, seeing myself in his dark, soulful eyes. "This is a lot harder than I thought it would be. But it's gotta be done. We're the only chance they have."

Tonka lies down on the seat to rest against my thigh. I take his change in mood to mean he believes me and knows I'll be OK. If anyone was around to hear me say that, they would probably say I'm projecting human qualities onto an animal. Some might say I'm crazy.

But you know what? I don't care. This little dog has become my best friend, my confidant, and my savior. He knows what I'm thinking and what I feel. If not for him, I'd be losing it right now. Of all the places Challenger might have ended up, it landed at his home. I don't know what forces brought us together, but I thank the heavens above for allowing it to happen. I'd be lost without him.

Comforted by these thoughts, I turn my focus back to our messed-up situation. Darkness comes fast when the days grow shorter, and there's no way we can make it back before nightfall. The golf cart has headlights, but the idea of driving through the wooded areas is risky. It's also unnecessary. We came prepared.

Returning to the closest house that wasn't flooded, I roll out the sleeping bag and make camp in its family room. It's dark by the time we've finished eating and we've had a long day. Tonka settles in beside me on the floor and I turn out the lantern.

CHAPTER EIGHT

Buddy and Baxter

Today, things go a lot different. Now that he has overcome his fear caused by the garage door incident, Tonka loves riding in the cart. It's like he was born to it. His ears stand at full alert, his nose twitches as he takes in unfamiliar scents, and his eyes scan the road ahead as we speed along.

But then, as we're going down a long stretch of open road, he blinks a few times and lies beside me, seeking shelter from the wind. I hadn't noticed at first, but I understand what's happening. The wind is drying out his eyes...and mine...and I kick myself for having destroyed the windshield. It really makes a difference. I recall reading...*there goes my selective memory thing again*...a dog's eyes are more sensitive than a human's. Catching a bug head-on could even cause blindness. I make a mental note to look out for another gas-powered golf cart.

After an hour, we've finished re-visiting all the houses with pets on my list. Now it's back to the grind of opening each new house we come to and listing things I might need later. Only this time, if there are pets inside, I let them go or leave the door open so they can get out later.

Sometimes this is trickier than it sounds. Some dogs are enormous...and aggressive. I know it's not their fault. They're hungry, confused and protecting their homes. But knowing that doesn't make them less of a threat to us.

So, I put my analytical brain to work again and come up with an idea. *I'm really loving this problem-solving talent I'm blessed with.* It only takes a few minutes to go back to the house where I commandeered the golf cart and remove a wire rope attached to one of the garage door's springs. My idea is to loop one end around the cart's back bumper, attach the other end to the door, and yank it open with the cart. Unlike the garage door incident, this scheme is going to work. I'm sure of it.

It doesn't take long to find out. The first house we come to upon resuming our break-ins has two dogs trapped inside. After hooking the cable to the door and the cart, I hit the gas like I'm Brittany Force blasting off the starting line in an NHRA dragster. Not only does my scheme work, the door, the frame, and part of the wall it's attached to come out with it! Booya! *Booya? Is that a thing?* OK. Maybe I'll take it a little slower next time.

Tonka and I watch from a distance, waiting for the dogs to leave and it's safe to go inside to take inventory. By lunch time, we've broken into a dozen homes and I'm feeling pretty good about our efforts. Time to break for lunch.

As I look over the map while eating an energy bar, I realize how daunting this task is. We have more than a hundred houses yet to explore in this section alone. Dozens more on the other side of the main road. After that, there are hundreds of houses between this community and town. How far can I take this?

And what about the rest of the state? The country? Am I really the only person left on the planet?

The answers in my head raise their hands like school kids saying, "Oooo! Pick me, pick me! I know!" But I refuse to let them speak to me. I don't like those answers. Those answers suck.

Instead, I pick up the accounting book, scanning the addresses and resources I've listed. There are pages and pages of addresses where tools, clothes, non-perishable foods and dog food are located. I've even listed firearms...not that there's anybody around to shoot even if they needed shooting. But if that ever changes, I'll know where to find the weapons to do it.

We have more supplies listed than we can use in five years. There's little point in continuing to open houses for food and other resources. It takes a lot of time and effort to open each door. And I can always resume searching later. Besides, the perishable foods, especially those left in the refrigerators, are stinking up the houses.

I know better than to open a fridge or freezer door. The gasses are toxic at this point and the smell unbearable. Even with the doors closed, the homes stink.

I decide to continue, but open only those places where pets are evident. Dogs always bark when I knock on the door. They're easy. Cats aren't so obvious, but there are usually clues. When I'm able to see the kitchen from outside and spot food and water bowls on the floor, there's a cat inside. If I don't see such signs, I move on to the next house.

But the longer we go on, the fewer pets we come across. The sad truth is, many of them have already perished from lack of food and water. If you've ever smelled a decaying animal on the side of the road, you can imagine what it smells like inside a closed-up house.

I hadn't thought about it before, but it's another good reason for freeing the animals. I'll be able to go back inside those homes when I need something. Those places where the animals didn't make it out...no way. It'll take years before the stench goes away.

This is gross stuff, I know. But this is my life now. It's imperative I take these things into consideration and plan for them. They never mentioned these details in the post-apocalypse movies and books. This is reality...and it reeks.

We move on to the next street to continue knocking on doors and looking through windows. It goes quick now because, like I said, we're finding fewer pets to release and we're not opening homes up to take inventory anymore.

We ride the golf cart to every house, so it's never far away. I don't want to risk getting separated from our food and water, and to be honest...I look at it as our get-away car. I don't know what we might need to get away from, but the little voice in my head says it's a good idea. You can't be too careful.

As the afternoon wears on, we come to the last house on a dead-end road. I knock on the front door and hear a weak, pitiful whine. By peering through the front door's glass pane, I'm able to see to the back of the house. On the floor in front of a sliding glass door in the kitchen...as though waiting to be let out...is a small mound of black fur. It has to be a dog!

I rush around the house and jimmy the door open with my crowbar. The graying face of a Scottish Terrier greets me with...I swear...a smile. He musters his strength to wag his tail and tries to stand, but fails. Grabbing a bowl sitting on the kitchen counter, I find the closest bathroom, rip off the lid to the toilet's tank, and fill the container with water.

I dash back to find Tonka sitting next to the Scottie, his eyes darting back and forth between the black terrier and me. His concern for the little fellow is both touching and telling. It rips at my heart. The Westie's dark eyes confirm my worst fears.

Lowering myself to the floor, I pull the Scottie onto my lap and hold the bowl up to his mouth so he can drink. He laps the water...once...twice...then turns to look at me with gratitude in his eyes. He struggles to push his little body up against mine, lets out a deep sigh, and goes limp.

The lump in my throat is so painful I fear I might pass out. An ache grips my heart and a wave of helplessness washes over me.

The handsome little fellow is gone...and I am done.

"I can't do this anymore!" I say aloud. "I did the best I can do, but I'm only one person! I can't save them all!"

As if seeing myself from a distance, I rise from the floor with the Scottie in my arms and place him on the countertop. I know I should cry or sob...but I'm numb. A million thoughts swirl through my head, but I can't grasp onto any of them.

Tonka paws at my leg, drawing me back from the blackness, and I remember my responsibilities. Regardless of what else is happening in this messed up world, it's up to me to protect and provide for my new best friend. And...I realize...in exchange he helps me hang on to my sanity. I don't think he's getting a fair trade.

The military-style trench tool I keep in the golf cart for emergencies isn't the best tool for the job I must do. But spotting the door to the garage, I leave the poor little Scottie safe on the counter to search for a real shovel. I have to bury him. Just leaving him here isn't an option.

When I open the door, I see an old black motorcycle with a sidecar in the middle of the garage. There are no cars, the space is dedicated to the bike. And no wonder. It's a classic vehicle. The garage itself is immaculate...painted floors, panels with hooks and shelves to hang tools, and a workbench along the outside wall. At the end of the bench next to the back door is a tool locker.

At the head of the room is a small bar with a flat-panel TV, refrigerator, and barstools. Prominently displayed behind the bar is a large poster of a man with a gray beard wearing a black leather jacket and old-style aviator goggles sitting on the motorcycle. Next to him in the sidecar sits a black Scottie, also wearing goggles. A caption at the bottom of the poster reads, "Buddy and Baxter—One Million Miles." It's not clear which one is which, but it seems likely Baxter is the dog.

Impressed, I take an admiring look at the bike and notice the goggles they're wearing on the poster are hanging from the handlebars. The man's leather coat is draped across the sidecar. I make a mental note to grab the goggles when we leave. They'll come in handy. A
quick look inside the locker scores me the shovel I need and several life vests for boating. One is made for a small dog. I make a note to grab it as well.

A few minutes later, I have a hole deep enough to bury the poor Scottie. It's a pleasant spot. The back of the house is really the front, as it faces a canal boaters used to access the community's inner harbor. Each house has its own dock, and the channel leads to a series of finger canals with more homes. Many of them still have boats moored to the docks, though some have sunk and others rest battered in the yards.

I retrieve the leather jacket from the bike, wrap it around Baxter, and place him in the makeshift grave. Tonka peers over the edge, paying his last respects to a fellow terrier. My eyes tear, but it's the only outward emotion I can muster.

"I think it would be right to say a prayer or something," I say, wiping my eyes with the back of my hand. "But I don't know the right words. If the poster is any indication, I'm sure he had a good and long life. He's one of the lucky ones. The pets we've released face a tough road. The ones we won't get to...I can't think about them. It's too hard."

As I shovel dirt back into the hole, I feel my heart hardening, turning to stone. I don't want to stop trying to release the pets...but I have to...for my own good. The few that have made it this long are too weak to survive. I don't know what happened to their owners, but I can't keep burying their beloved pets or my heart truly will turn to stone...and I'll never feel anything again.

CHAPTER NINE

The Land Road

"It's a simple concept," I say to Tonka as I separate my hair into three equal sections. "But not such a simple thing to achieve. I've seen enough of the main road to know we'll have to deal with a lot of fallen trees. A chainsaw is a must. Fortunately, we already have one and the right gas to go with it."

The terrier, in his all-knowing way, looks at me with dark eyes that say he's not sure this is a great idea.

"Yeah, it'll be hard, but I have to try. For all I know, there are other survivors there. Maybe they can't come to us. So, we're going to go to them."

The Westie licks the remains of the morning meal off his face and burps his objection. He's not convinced.

"Look," I say, annoyed, "I'm not going to just sit here waiting, hoping somebody shows up. I have to do something. I need to find out how far this rapture thing goes. Besides, I'm not ready to believe I'm the only person left on earth. I mean, me? Out of all the people in the world? How stupid would that be?"

Tonka perks up at this, seeming to agree, and I wonder if I should be insulted? Can dogs do sarcasm? Ignoring the insult, I turn my attention to outfitting the golf cart for our next excursion.

I feel a little better today. We made it back to Tonka's house before dark and, after starting a fire in the woodstove, I made chili from a steak I found in the freezer. It was fantastic! I don't know how I know how to cook, but I do. Just more selective memory weirdness.

After taking a shower, I spent about an hour combing the knots out of my hair. Riding around in a golf cart with no windshield wreaked havoc on my unbound tresses. Detangling the bird's nest of a mess was *no fun at all.*

While working out the knots, I focused on dealing with the day's epiphany. *That's a big word. Do I know it because I'm a faith-based person or just nerding out again?* I know I can't go on releasing pets...that's settled. For the sake of my heart and my sanity, I deem this task as done. By the time I went to bed, my mind was made up about two things. First, it's time to move on to the next task...to go to town. And second, to weave my hair into a French braid like Lara Croft. I may not be raiding tombs, but given the challenges I face, I might as well be. Tomb Raider knew what she was doing! *Lara Croft? Tomb Raider? Am I a gamer? I hope I'm not one of those people who spends all her time playing video games!*

My plan for today is to make our way up Broad Creek Road...the only way off the peninsula...to where it connects to Highway 55. About two miles from this intersection, the road merges into Highway 17. It then crosses the river into town. I have no idea how long it will take to reach the end of Broad Creek Road. It could be half a day. Maybe half a week. It depends on how many trees have fallen across the two lanes and how big they are.

Resupplying the cart is easy. Most of what we need is already loaded, left from our last outing. Other than adding more food and water, all we need is a siphon hose.

Yeah, I need a hose to drain gas from cars and trucks so I can fill up the golf cart. Of course, nobody keeps siphon hoses around, but it's easy to make one. I just cut the ends off a six-foot garden hose and...voila! A siphon hose. Easy peasy, lemon squeezy.

After topping off the cart's gas tank using fuel from a neighbor's car, we're off. It's a sunny day, but the air is brisk and once again I chastise myself for having broken the windshield. On the positive side, we now have goggles to protect our eyes from airborne hazards. They also help protect against the cold.

It's fortunate Tonka doesn't balk at wearing the goggles at all. OK, maybe a little. He paws at them a few times as though saying, "Get this dang thing off my face!" But, as the cart speeds up, he understands the wind isn't messing with his eyes anymore. He's an incredible dog. And now he's loving the open-air ride.

I know from the map the distance to Highway 55 is eight miles. The speedometer shows we are going just over twenty-five miles per hour. Simple math tells me we can make it to the highway in about twenty minutes...unless there is a tree laying across the road.

And there it is. We haven't even gone a mile when we come to a gigantic pine tree crossing both lanes. Water surrounds the tree's broken trunk. The top extends past a gully parallel to the road. In other words, there's no way to drive around the darn thing.

"OK, little buddy," I say, retrieving the chainsaw from the back of the cart. "Cover your ears. It's time to crank this sucker up."

I don't know if I've ever used a chainsaw before, but the controls are pretty straightforward. Set the throttle to choke, pull the cord. If it doesn't start, pull the cord again. When it starts, I leave the choke on until it coughs, then I move the throttle to the run position. Easy pea... Never mind. I leave the saw running while I put on a pair of earmuffs and...using my goggles for eye protection...I go to work.

Right away, I figure out I have to cut out small sections so they're not too heavy for me to handle. Instead of logs, the sections look more like the wheels on Fred Flintstone's car. Thirty minutes later, I've cut a gap wide enough to drive the cart through.

"Not bad," I say to Tonka, who's lying on the cart's seat. "But there's got to be a faster way. I'm making too many cuts and taking too much time."

After returning the saw to the back of the cart, we continue on. I'm still mentally patting myself on the back and feeling pretty good about our progress when, two minutes later, we come upon another fallen tree. Unbelievable! This tree is bigger than the first one! My heart sinks a little, but it's not like I didn't expect it. Time to toughen up, Princess Buttercup.

Before starting the saw, I take the slack out of the chain using a handy tool clipped to its casing. The funny thing is, I didn't realize I was doing basic saw maintenance until I was done. Maybe I have used a chainsaw before.

On the upside, it only takes half as long to cut an opening as it did the first time. Why? Because, before starting, I take a minute to think things through. It's amazing what a girl can accomplish if she engages her brain first. Instead of making seven or eight narrow cutouts, I make one wide one. Then I wrap the steel rope around the cutout and pull it away with the cart. Easy peasy, lemon squeezy. *I'm really hating that phrase, but I guess I'm going to have to learn to live with it.*

All in all, things aren't going bad. It might take a while, but as long as the chainsaw keeps running, I know we'll make it to the main highway. Eventually. Once again, I stow away the saw and drive on.

We make pretty good time for the next five or six minutes, but it's not all clear sailing. We come across several more fallen trees but manage to go around them. At some point, I'll need to come back and cut a path through them so as not to risk getting stuck or breaking an axle. The off-road terrain can be rough. But that will have to wait until later. Right now, I'm too excited to stop if I don't have to.

Taking a quick glance at the map, I see we are about three miles from the main highway now. I'm not sure, but the fact there aren't any buildings along this section of the road makes me believe we're passing through a state-owned park. Or maybe a forest kept up by a hunting club. The woods on either side of the road are well-maintained and cleared of underbrush. Charring at the base of the trees shows there had been a recent controlled burn. It's weird to see virgin woodland with almost no undergrowth.

Despite the easy going, my senses are on full alert for any signs of trouble. This isn't like driving to the corner grocery store. Not that I'm old enough to have a driver's license. At least, I don't think I am. I have no idea what might be around the next corner. And as soon as the thought pops into my head, I find out.

A giant pine blocking the road forces us to stop. This thing is humongous! It's twice as big as the others. I had no idea pine trees could grow so big. And, of course, there's no way to go around it. Sigh... This is going to be a big job.

The chainsaw I have is small. The blade is only sixteen inches long. It's light enough for me to handle, but not the best tool for a big job. The trunk of this tree is like six feet in diameter. Seriously. I can't even see over the top of it. It's stupid big. The only way to cut through it with this saw is to carve out small chunks at a time.

"Well, make yourself comfortable," I say to Tonka as I fill the saw's gas tank. "This is going to take a while."

He settles into the seat, his head resting on his paws so he can watch me while I work.

The air is cool, so I'm not worried about working up a serious sweat...or perspiration if you insist. It's a girl thing. Still, after a few minutes, I have to take a break to remove the chambray shirt I'm wearing over the wife-beater T-shirt I found in one of the vacation condos. I despise the name, but love the tank top. Anyway, I toss the shirt on the seat next to Tonka and get back to work.

The air is brisk, but the sun on my bare arms feels good. The smell of fresh-cut pine and chainsaw exhaust fills the air. It's not an unpleasant combination. I think I could develop a fondness for this lumberjill thing. Maybe try out for the Ax Women of Maine and go on the state fair circuit.

How in the wide world of Carmen Sandiego do I know about the Ax Women of Maine? I am SO weird.

As I bend over to start the saw, I see Tonka from the corner of my eye standing on the seat, looking back down the road from where we've come. His hackles are up, and his upper lip is curled in a snarl like he's growling at something...but there's no sound. Have I lost my hearing?!

The bizarre thought evaporates with the realization I'm still wearing earmuffs. Stupid, stupid, stupid me! As I remove the muffs, I spot the thing that's switched on Tonka's protective beast mode. In the middle of the road half a football field away is something large, black and furry. It's a freakin' bear!

Panic shoots through my body like fifty-thousand watts of ice-cold electricity. OK, I know that makes little sense...but that's the way it feels. It's more than fear. It's the undeniable fact we're trapped! We can't go forward because of the tree, and we can't go back because we'd be going toward the bear. And then, just to add a healthy serving of terror into the mix, the huge bruin rises to stand on his hind legs while staring straight at us.

Did I say it's a big bear? That's not accurate. It's not just big. Oh, no, of course not. This must be the biggest black bear in the history of bears! A new species I dub Ursus Americanus Giganticus. *Geez...now I'm doing animal taxonomy?* There's no way this can be any worse.

It's at this moment I realize I haven't been to the bathroom in like, for-ev-er. On top of everything else, I'm scared I'll wet my pants. As stupid as it might sound, given the circumstances, I fear somebody will find my mangled body in the middle of the road and all they'll notice is I peed my pants. Laugh if you want, but girls think about these things.

Somehow, the absurd notion counters my panic, and my brain engages. With a speed I didn't know I possessed, I grab my shirt off the seat, tie one sleeve to Tonka's collar and the other to the seat's hip bar. I hate doing it, but I just know this crazy dog will try to attack the bear if it comes any closer.

Next, I grab the chainsaw and yank the starter cord with everything I've got. The engine fires up and I say a silent prayer of thanks. Holding it over my head with both hands, I rev the engine as high as it will go.

The bear takes a couple of steps toward us, looking way more mad than scared. NOT the response I was going for. I rev the engine over and over like a mad motorcyclist and Tonka joins in with a tirade of barks.

The bear drops to all fours and starts towards us at a fast gait. Somehow, I manage to hold my water as I slide behind the steering wheel and start the engine. Forget rational thinking. I'm running on instinct now. Our only hope is to be aggressive.

With the gas pedal pushed to the floorboard and the screaming chainsaw held outside the cart with my left hand, I steer us on a collision course toward the charging bear. The idea of turning the wheel at the last moment and sideswiping the bear with the saw flashes through my mind. It's not a brilliant plan, but it's all I've got.

I'm so focused on the giant bruin, I'm not paying attention to the road. The front tire on the passenger's side hits a limb, yanking the cart into a hard right turn. Momentum rips the saw from my hand and the machine bounces across the pavement a couple of times before coming to a stop, landing upright. At the same time, I hit the brake to keep the cart from sliding into the ditch.

By some weird quirk of fate, the chainsaw is still running, creating a sputtering, smoking obstacle between us and the bear. Ursus Giganticus stops in front of the saw as the engine's vibrations send it dancing atop the pavement in random directions. He looks at the rattling machine like it's a demented alien predator and takes several wary steps to go around it. He's being cautious, but he's not giving up on eating us.

As the bear circles counterclockwise around the saw to come up behind us, I stomp on the gas pedal and steer the cart back onto the road. He sees we're getting away and breaks into a dead run. Tonka, with his front paws braced on the back of the seat, is barking at the bear for all he's worth.

This time, I stay focused on the road, making sure I don't hit something else. In the back of my mind, I'm trying to remember how fast a black bear can run. Is it thirty miles an hour or thirty-five? Why I would know such information, I have no idea. It's a little nuts, for sure. As the sound of the chainsaw engine fades, I start to breathe easier. It looks like we're going to get away.

A glance in the cart's side-view mirror dashes this notion all to smithereens. The bear is gaining on us! At least now I have the answer to my question. I don't know about the average black bear, but this one can run faster than thirty-five.

I look ahead just in time to see a pile of debris in the road and swerve around it. The bear lunges at the cart but misses because of our sudden change of direction. In baseball parlance, this is known as a swing and a miss. *And no, I have no idea how I know baseball stuff either!* Another glance in the mirror and I see the bear tumbling into the ditch. The momentum of grabbing empty air instead of the cart tripped him up. It may have been dumb luck that saved us, but I'll take any luck I can get.

By now, I'm crossing my legs as hard as I can, but there's no way I'm going to stop. I need to put as much space between us and the bear as possible in case he resumes the chase. It's only after a couple of miles when we pass through one of the carved-out trees I dare to pull over. I have to or else I really am going to wet my pants. Seriously, I need to go so bad I feel it in my back teeth.

I get my pants down just in time and manage to relieve myself while keeping an eye up the road. There's no dignity in what I'm doing. If anybody could see me, I'd be embarrassed beyond belief. But I don't care. Nature didn't just call. It snuck up on me, threw me to the ground, and jumped up and down on my full bladder with both feet. And that's all I'm gonna say about that.

75

Chapter Ten

Käfer Mist

As we resume our trip back to the cottage, Tonka stands on the seat with his front legs braced apart and his chest puffed out, ready to take on any and all threats. I'm convinced he believes he's a bulldog or a rottweiler. I wonder if he looks more intimidating to other animals with the goggles on. Like Cyclops in the X-Men movies. There's no doubt in my mind he would have attacked the bear if I hadn't tied him down with my shirt. I still believe it's better to leave him unleashed most of the time. But I make a mental note to keep a leash in the cart from now on. Just in case.

As for me...I'm still shaking. If not for a lucky accident, I'd be mincemeat. And it was my fault. I was unprepared, a circumstance I resent to my core. I'm smarter than that, but I allowed my emotions to overrule my common sense. I opted not to carry a weapon because of a misguided notion. The idea I don't need one because there aren't any people couldn't be more wrong. I almost paid for this faulty logic with my life. Trust me, it's a mistake I won't make again.

As the trembling subsides, my thoughts turn to bigger issues like, how am I going to make it to town? I'm not saying I won't go out on the road again. I refuse to surrender to fear. I just won't. But it will be a while before I leave my back uncovered while using a chainsaw. Being unable to see a threat is bad enough. Not being able to hear it is a double whammy...and far too dangerous. At least for now. I mean, we're talking freakin' bears here! The idea bears would be an issue never crossed my mind.

Several schemes run through my mind, like somehow setting up mirrors so I can see behind me while sawing. Or maybe stopping the saw every minute or two to check around me. But those ideas create other problems. And for all I know, the bears associate chainsaw noise with food left by loggers. So maybe running the saw will attract them no matter what I do.

"Geez, Louise!" I say. "This is like Chinese math. There's got to be a way. I need to know if any people in town survived."

Tonka's ears twitch, so I know he hears me. But he continues to scan the road ahead, ever the diligent scout.

It's at least an hour before dark when we make it back. It's weird to have time to kill, so I use it to explore the house again, something I haven't done since I first arrived. I find nothing new, but when I spot the PC upstairs, an idea hits me. There's no Internet, but maybe it has a game like Klondike or Tetris I can play.

Surprise! When I open the guest portal, I see dozens of folders on the splash page. Whoever owned the computer loaded it with programs and files like *Merriam-Webster Dictionary*, *World Book Encyclopedia*, *Atlas Maps of the World*, *World Geography Challenge*, *Gray's Anatomy*, *Space Atlas*, about twenty years of *Mother Earth News*, *Emergency Medicine*, on and on. There are even three different versions of the *Holy Bible* and entries for a dozen more religions.

"Wow!" I say to Tonka, who's lying on my feet. "This computer is the equivalent of a research library. The people who live here must be survivalists or something. It also contains files with tons of music, movies, and a boatload of e-novels. And speaking of boats, it has files on sailing and navigation. What a find!"

How nuts would it have been to have all these resources at my fingertips and never found them? I didn't turn the computer on before because I thought the homeowners were returning. Besides, with the entire grid out, the Internet doesn't function. Not only do I have an indispensable library of reference books, I have enough novels, games and music to keep me entertained for years. The hard drive on this thing is at least twenty terabytes!

A wave of computer knowledge and terms flood my consciousness like an Indonesian tsunami. I'm not just a geek, I'm the whole squad.

I push the chair back and stare at the screen. Between reclaiming a huge portion of useful memories and finding a treasure trove of knowledge, I'm gobsmacked! On the other hand, I could spend hours going through all this information and it wouldn't help me solve my problem…how to get to town.

Or can it?

Guided by intuition, I open the encyclopedia folder and find the subfiles starting with the letter N. Not only am I surprised by how much information about this town is available, I discover I possess the attention span of goldfish.

The entry on "New Bern" explains the river town was named after the city of Bern in Switzerland. Well, duh. But as I said, my newly discovered proclivity to be distracted by figurative shiny objects has kicked into overdrive. Having been informed of the obvious,

I'm compelled to open the B entries to learn more about the original Bern.

This article documents the city of Bern as being founded in 1191 by some dude named Berchtold the Fifth, the Duke of Zähringen. Huh? So now I gotta look up Zähringen because...well, what girl would choose to go through life not knowing where Zähringen is?

It turns out, Zähringen was a noble German family and took its name from a castle near "Freiburg im Breisgau, Baden." Well...isn't that special? Come on, pointy-headed encyclopedia writers! Tell me how the castle got *its* name?

Another ten minutes of research reveals zip. Nothing. I guess nobles in the twelfth century were keen on naming themselves after inanimate objects, but when it came to documenting the origins of words, not so much.

Aggravated that I will forever remain ignorant as to what Zähringen means, I go back to the previous file to learn more about the local folklore...the folklore of Bern, that is. So, if the residents back then are to be believed...and I see no reason they shouldn't be...Duke Zaggernut as I will forever call him...decided to build a city and vowed to name it after the first animal he killed in the area where it was to be built.

And the winner was...drum roll please...a bear. No kidding, Bern means bear. Good thing for the residents of Bern good ol' Duke Zaggernut didn't step on a dung beetle or something. Of course, now I have to look up the Swiss word for dung beetle. And, not too surprising at this point, I find folders for all kinds of language translation dictionaries. I open the one titled Swiss-German to English.

"Käfer Mist!" I say aloud and begin snorting like an asthmatic bloodhound with the hiccups. Annoyed, Tonka gives me a half-growl, half-grunt, then turns his head to face the wall.

Nice. If there are any dukes out there wanting to name a city, I humbly offer the name Käfer Mist. I'm confident the Swiss word for dung beetle has yet to be claimed by any other city on the planet. If, however, this turns out not to be true, I have an easy fix. Simply name the town *New* Käfer Mist. You're welcome.

It's fun to laugh again, even if it's at myself. The day's frustrations and anxiety fall away like scales, and I feel better than I have since the storm. Doing research like this is not only therapeutic, it's like coming home to something familiar. I seem to have a built-in thirst for knowledge, and I like it.

It's getting late and we need to eat before calling it a day, but I want to look up one more thing. Switching back to the tab on New Bern, I scroll to a section on fauna and find an entry on bears. I don't need a color-coded range map to verify the existence of bears around here. It's something I've already done, up close and way too personal. What I want to know is how abundant they are.

Confirming my suspicion, the entry says Craven County, where New Bern is located, and the surrounding counties, are home to hundreds if not thousands of black bears. Bear sightings occur almost every day. Collisions with cars and trucks are reported several times a year. In addition, because of its name and the enormous population of Ursus Americanus, residents often refer to their city as Bear Town.

The article also says, when bears are feeding during the summer to put on fat, people are advised to bring in their bird feeders at night and to secure their garbage cans so bears can't get to them. And whatever you do, don't leave Rover outside...that bark you hear in the middle of the night might be his last.

Yikes!

I look at Tonka and shiver. If Ursus Giganticus had grabbed him, my poor Westie would have been gone in two gulps. I'm definitely putting a leash in the cart.

As I'm about to close the tab, a note at the bottom of the page catches my eye. It's a warning about other threats residents should be concerned about.

"For information about other carnivores in Eastern North Carolina such as alligators, coyotes and the recently re-introduced red wolf, click here."

You have *got* to be kidding me! You mean we have to watch out for alligators, bears, coyotes *and* red wolves? And I haven't even looked up venomous snakes yet.

To say I was already concerned is an understatement. This takes things to a whole new level. I won't be chancing it by sawing through fallen trees any time soon, that's for sure. And from now on, I'll literally be loaded for bear when we leave the house. Becoming the main course for a starving predator is *not* on my bucket list.

This girl isn't stupid and I'm not a wuss. If I'm going down, I'm going down fighting. And that's all there is to it.

CHAPTER ELEVEN

Plan B

After breakfast, I have one priority...return to houses I've listed where weapons and ammunition are stored. Not every house. Only the ones with what I need. So, how do I decide exactly what it is I need? By checking my firearms knowledge on the computer, of course.

Once I decided to arm myself, my dormant memories bubbled up like a carbon dioxide and diet cola cocktail. It turns out I know a lot about guns and ammunition. And according to the computer, I've got it right. The two weapons I decide on are an AR-15 rifle chambered for 5.56-millimeter ammo and a 9-

millimeter handgun. A rifle designed to shoot 5.56 rounds can safely fire a .223-inch round, but not the reverse. Being able to fire two different-sized rounds means there's a lot more ammo available than would be otherwise.

Also, the rounds are smaller than those made for large caliber rifles. There are two other advantages to this. Smaller ammunition means less recoil. I like my shoulder to remain unbruised, thank you very much. And, the ammo weighs less, so I can carry more if I need to. Not that I want to, but you never know.

Of course, there's always a tradeoff when making such choices. An AR-15 probably won't drop a bear with one shot. But it's big enough to make him rethink attacking me. And with an AR-15, I'll have at least nineteen more rounds to fire if the first one doesn't convince him to leave me alone.

I also need a weapon I can carry hands-free. The 9-millimeter pistol is a no-brainer for me. It has less recoil than bigger caliber handguns and is a weapon I can shoot with one hand. The 9-millimeter is a popular caliber, which means ammo is easier to find.

How do I know this stuff? I have no idea. Like my computer knowledge, it's just there in my brain. I retain the information, but I don't know why or how it got in my head. The more research I do to check myself, the more confident I am I know what I'm doing. That's a big deal with firearms. Safety is paramount!

Another thing I realize is how weirdly selective my memory is. I don't remember specific things about myself. But when it comes to general information about the world and life, I'm a fountain of knowledge. I'm just not aware it's in my head until I need it. For instance, I know a lot of people freak out about firearms. Guns should never be taken lightly, but this is the world I live in now. This is about life and death. My life and my death. If I'm killed by a bear or a wolf, I don't get to come back to life like a video game character. This is real. Dying is permanent. I'm not taking any chances.

And while it would be cool to have a bow as my weapon of choice, I'm not Katniss Everdeen and I can't shoot an arrow through an apple in a roasted pig's mouth a hundred paces away. At least, I don't think I can. I may want to try it later. Who am I kidding? Of course I will. But firearms are the best option for protecting Tonka and me from threats, especially from a distance.

Firearms are also a better choice because they make a loud noise when fired. Maybe firing a warning shot will be enough to scare away a big predator. Not wounding or killing an animal when there's no need to is the best outcome. It's an option arrows don't afford.

Picking up the weapons, ammunition and a pair of shooter's earmuffs doesn't take long, thanks to the inventory logs I've kept. By mid-morning, I'm setting up a shooting range on the street in front of Tonka's house. With cul-de-sacs at both ends and no houses at the far end of the street, I can shoot the long gun without fear of damaging someone's home. If the rounds don't hit a tree, they'll carry out to the river and fall into the water. No worries.

I'm fortunate the AR-15 I recovered is equipped with a red-dot scope. This means I can zero the sight with the target just fifty yards away. Not to get too technical, but given the ballistic characteristics of 5.56 ammo, a rifle zeroed at fifty yards is also zeroed for two hundred yards...or close enough. And, with a red dot scope, it's a lot easier to sight a target at fifty yards than it is at two hundred.

To stabilize the rifle, I use pillows from the house and bags from a corn hole game and prop it up on a card table. I pace off fifty yards and tape my target...the flap of a cardboard box with a black magic marker X sketched across it...onto a six-foot stepladder. I take a seat on a folding chair behind the table, put on the earmuffs, take aim, exhale, and squeeze off the first round.

Poor Tonka! My terrier friend has probably never heard a gun being fired. Even though he was fifty feet away, the bang sends him scurrying up the steps to the front door. I rush to him in a panic and find him huddled up in a ball, shaking.

"Why?!" I say. "Why can't I remember to think things through?"

Tonka hears my voice, lifts his head and looks at me with a face that asks, "Is it OK to come out?"

I scoop him up in my arms and go inside, then rub him until he stops shaking. When he's calmed down, I give him a rawhide to chew, hoping it will help relieve his tension.

"I hate doing this to you," I say, stroking the top of his head, "but I have to make sure these weapons fire true. Heck, I need to know they work, period. I can't chance waiting until I need them to find out they don't fire."

Tonka continues gnawing on the rawhide, ignoring me. Good. Now I know he's OK, I can go back to work.

I return to the table and sit behind the rifle. Before firing, I glance toward the house and see Tonka watching me through a front window. I fire my second round of the day and pause to see if he's still watching.

Yes! He didn't panic this time, so I cross my fingers and hope this means he's associating the blast of the gun with me, making the noise OK. Eventually, I'll bring him out on the front porch where he'll be closer to the noise, yet still feel safe. It might take time, but he needs to be comfortable around guns and shooting. If breeds like setters and pointers can learn this, why not West Highland White Terriers? They're hunting dogs, too.

At least now I can focus on zeroing the weapons. I fire a third round, then walk to the target. All three rounds missed the bullseye two inches to the left. Not bad, but not perfect. On the good side, the three shots made a nice tight group.

Now, back at the table, I adjust the scope's red dot to the shot-group's center. I then readjust the rifle on the bags so the red dot is on the bullseye and fire three more rounds. The bullets punch out the center of the X.

Booya!

The handgun I've commandeered is a military-style 9-millimeter semi-automatic with a seventeen-round magazine. Though not adjustable, the sights have tritium dots for aiming in the dark. Tritium is the radioactive material used to illuminate traffic signs and the numbers on analog watches. I hope I never have to shoot at night, but if I do, at least I'll be able to aim.

I make another cardboard target and move the ladder closer to the table. Next, I brace my hands on the pile of corn hole bags and fire three rounds. The handgun fires high, but not enough to worry about. If I need to shoot something up close, it will be hard to miss.

Satisfied my weapons fire true, I take them apart and clean them. A clean weapon is less likely to jam. Knowing how to fire them isn't enough. I have to be comfortable shooting them under pressure, even at night. And if something goes wrong, I'll need to take them apart without thinking.

It's lunchtime, so I break long enough to check on Tonka and eat a can of beanie weenies. His eyes narrow when he sees the weapons, but doesn't freak out. What a relief!

Now it's time for the next step of Plan B. After strapping the handgun to my thigh in a sweet leather holster a la Lara Croft, I mount a rifle case to the golf cart. I've modified it to function like the rifle scabbards cowboys use with horses. It's set up so I can grab the AR-15 with one hand while sitting behind the steering wheel. I don't know if saving a few seconds will make a difference, but I'm not taking anything for granted.

Ready, Freddy? Here we come!

The drive to the marina where the lightning struck is quick and easy. No bears, no coyotes, no alligators. Easy peasy. Tonka and I leave the cart in the parking lot and scope out sailboats undamaged by the storm. I need something small...I'm only one girl...and I need it to have a retractable keel.

My hope is to find a boat with a draft shallow enough to navigate the creek behind Tonka's house. This means it has to be a sailboat, not a powerboat. If a powerboat runs out of gas or the engine malfunctions, we'd be stranded with no one to call for help. A sailboat with a small engine means we can move no matter what. Also, the small engine on a sailboat uses less gas than a powerboat...an important consideration given my gasoline will have to be siphoned from other boats.

We start our search at the docks on the outside piers. The closer the boat is to the open water, the better. The closer it is to the main dock, the harder it will be to navigate through the maze of piers and wrecked boats.

It takes only a few minutes to see the fallacy of my logic. The outside slips are where the bigger boats are docked. These slips are the closest to the open water, so they took the hardest pounding and suffered the most damage.

Time to reverse my logic. We go back to the dock closest to land and start our search anew. The boats that still look seaworthy are too big. The boats that aren't too big are too damaged. I'm about to give up when...there she is! A Parker 235 mini-cruiser! Riding high in the water, undamaged, and the perfect size. Yes! Yes! And yes!

Knowledge floods my consciousness like water rushing from a busted dam. The Parker, a British-built sailboat, is twenty-three-and-a-half-feet long, has a retractable keel...or as the Brits would say, a lifting keel...a six-horsepower engine, four berths, and a mini-galley. Best of all...it has a head. Having a private place to go is important. It's a girl thing.

I see the boat's name on the stern and can't help but chuckle. In big block letters, it says, TITANIC II— ICEBREAKER. It's a British boat, and with a name like that, it's probably owned by a Brit. They're known for having a dry sense of humor.

What makes this boat so perfect? When the keel is up, the boat draws only a foot of water...which means the hull won't hit bottom...as long as there's at least thirteen inches of water. It's like I just won the lottery. I couldn't have ordered a better boat.

As my brain processes the data dump, I stare at the sailboat, transfixed. It's hard to explain. It's like both hemispheres are operating at the same time. The left hemisphere recalls facts and figures about the boat. The right hemisphere imagines the tranquility of sailing upriver to town. Fuel economy, distances, water capacity, food storage, and navigation facts on the left side. On the right, visions of adventure, the wind blowing in my hair, the taste of salt in the air, the beauty of tropical sunsets and the exhilaration of being free.

Tonka pokes my leg with his paw, breaking the trance. It's obvious he's concerned and is asking, "Are you OK? Where did you go?"

I'm certain he knows things about me I don't. I can feel it in my bones. Dropping to the planks, I sit next to him and take him into my lap.

"I wish you could talk," I say for the hundredth time. "Sometimes I believe you can, but holding back, waiting for the right moment."

Of course, he doesn't reply and never will. The thought makes me wonder if I will ever hear a human's voice again.

"All the more reason we have to go to town," I say, putting Tonka down so I can stand. "I have to find out if other people are there...or anywhere."

Tonka watches from the dock as I step onto the boat to see if she is seaworthy. Like magic, a mental checklist for boating safety pops up from my latent memory. *Weird, but I'll take it.* I have to make sure there are two anchors, the water and gas tanks are full, and the sails, lines, pulleys, and winches are in working order. I also make sure the engine runs and there's a life vest my size.

At the end of the inspection, I come across a small pull-out table with a chart of local waters clipped to it. Sweet! It shows everything between Oriental...a small town downriver...and a train trestle upriver past New Bern. I also see Tonka's house is just a couple of miles away by water.

Everything checks out fine, and I make a mental note to add the canine life vest we commandeered from Buster and Baxter's house on the next trip. We have plenty of time before sunset, so we drive home, then walk back to the marina. Tonka balks when I make him wear Baxter's life vest. But after a couple of minutes and a dog treat, he doesn't seem to mind at all. He's a good sport.

Once we clear the marina, I cut the engine, drop the keel, and raise the mainsail. The little boat isn't very fast, but it sails like a dream. As I work the rudder and manipulate sail rigging, I'm certain I've done this before. It's all so familiar. Maybe not in a small cruiser like this, but I definitely know my way around sailboats.

CHAPTER TWELVE

The Water Road

Tonka waits on the dock as I move the food and other supplies from the golf cart to the sailboat. After waking early, we ate a quick breakfast and began the final preparations for our voyage. The sun is rising above the treetops on the far side of Broad Creek and its warmth on my face is reassuring.

But the air is much colder today, and it will be a while before I'm ready to shed the coat I'm wearing. At least, I hope it will warm up enough to lose the coat. I'm not ready for the cold of winter...the weather may have other ideas.

Once again, I strap Tonka into the canine life vest and lift him into the boat. The vest has a convenient padded strap sewn into its back panel, making it easy to lift the Westie. He grunts at me but is otherwise at ease being on the cruiser again. I thank the stars for small blessings. It's going to be a long day.

After starting the small outboard engine, I uncleat the mooring lines and shove off. The creek's water level is lower than yesterday, and the engine's prop kicks up the muddy bottom. The smells of decomposing marsh grass and other organic matter fill the air, but the boat chugs along OK. About a hundred feet from the dock, the water deepens, and I take a moment to look back at Tonka's home.

The sun's rays shining on the water's cool surface create a mist, making the little house appear more like a mirage than a solid dwelling. For the first time, I wonder at the perfect circumstance of its existence. It provides us shelter, warmth and conveniences no other place in the area can. And then I realize it's not just Tonka's home anymore, it's my home as well. Or it will be if we don't find people in town.

As we leave the narrow creek and enter deeper water, a pang of fear punches me in the gut. What if something happens to the house while I'm gone? What if something happens to the sailboat and we're stranded somewhere? What if we do find people in town, but they've turned into walkers...like on The Walking Dead?

The thought makes me laugh out loud, prompting Tonka to give me one of his "What now?" looks.

"OK, that's stupid," I say, rubbing the Westie's head to reassure him...and me. "It's time for me to channel my inner Jordan Turpin and get a grip on my fears."

Where the heck did that memory come from?

As I pause to stop the engine, drop the keel, and raise the sails, I think about the seventeen-year-old girl who escaped a life in captivity imposed by her parents. She had only been outside a handful of times in her entire life. She didn't even know how street signs worked. Despite knowing her parents would literally kill her if they found her before she found the police, she crawled through her bedroom window and made a 9-1-1 call that saved her and her twelve brothers and sisters from brutal beatings, starvation and death. She's the bravest person I've ever known, and I will forever look to her as my hero...or shero...as I like to say.

Once again, the selective nature of my memory taunts me. Why is it I can remember disturbing details about someone I've never met, yet I can't even remember my name? Or maybe I have met Jordan, but can only remember her story now? Somehow, I understand if I dwell on this weird paradox for long, it will drive me crazy.

Letting out a deep sigh, I resolve to quit fretting over the mystery of my selective memory and trust it will resolve itself...eventually. In the meantime, if a seventeen-year-old Jordan Turpin can save herself and her siblings, I can at least maintain the nerve to save myself. If I muster half the strength she had, I can do anything.

Sailing the Parker is a breeze…no pun intended. It's not just that she's a sweet little sailboat, the Neuse is a wide river with deep-water channels. Markers guide me to the river's far side, about a mile from the marina where I commandeered the boat. With the keel down, we need to keep the boat in at least six feet of water to avoid hitting bottom. And thanks to the chart I found, I can see where the deep water ends and the shallow water begins. This will be essential information when I reach town. Until then, I just need to follow the channel markers.

The wind is coming from the southeast, so the sailing is easy. My only tasks are to keep the mainsail trimmed and a hand on the rudder. To make the most of my time, I study the landscape on both sides of the river, making mental notes of landmarks and other features.

Even though the eastern bank is a mile away, I can see it's undeveloped. Nothing but trees and cattails. Not even the harbor community and the marina where I commandeered the boat reach the riverbank. The marina is tucked into a creek that flows into the river.

The river's west bank, the side we're on now, is much different. It has high bluffs with many houses built along the edges to take advantage of the sweeping view. The river is eating away the base of the bluffs. Houses once built farther back from the edge are now at risk of falling into the water. One day, they will.

Though sailing against the current, we're making good time. I'm so preoccupied with surveying the houses and landscape, I'm not paying attention to the open river in front of me. So it's a shock when I look up to see a large, two-masted schooner bearing down on us. Had the boat's sails been raised, I would have noticed it far sooner, but they aren't. Is it running on engine power? Are people on board?!

I veer to starboard, avoiding a head-on collision by inches. As we pass each other, I scan the boat's deck and helm for people. But there's no one. A glance at the front of the boat confirms my theory. The heavy bow line trails in the water, which means the schooner broke anchor and is flowing with the current. It is a ghost ship and will continue its journey until it reaches the sea. The joy of believing I'd found other people fades with the drifting boat.

Though I sigh in frustration, I follow it with a deep breath of resolve. I won't allow this disappointment to determine my mood for the day. We are alive and the beckoning river town lies ahead. There is hope.

After an hour of steady sailing, we reach the incredible high-rise bridges spanning the Neuse. Instead of making one bridge wide enough to handle four lanes, the engineers built two separate structures, each one accommodating two lanes. I don't understand why it was constructed this way. There must be a reason. Someday I may try to figure it out.

A look at the chart shows the twin bridges span two rivers, the Neuse and the Trent. Our destination is the point where these two rivers meet...a place named Union Point. It's the easternmost border of the town and...if the chart is correct...the location of public docks where we can moor the boat.

Appearing as double humps at our end of the twin spans, the bridges loom above my head some sixty-five or seventy feet high. The channel we're following flows under the bridge humps. The design allows sailboats with their tall masts to pass under the bridges where the water is deepest. This...my selective memory informs me...eliminates the need for draw bridges or swing bridges, allowing both the vehicles above and the boats on the river to pass freely.

As we sail under the bridge humps, I can't resist the urge to let out a blast on the boat's foghorn. Hundreds of seagulls scream their anger at having their peace disturbed, scaring the bejeebers out of us both. They flee their perches in a choreographed whirlwind of white...then glide back around to return to the ledges they had departed.

Any other time, it would have been fascinating. This time, however, I chastise myself for my stupidity. My thoughtless impulse may have alerted people in town...if there are any...that we are coming.

"Yes," I say to Tonka, my voice laced with the aggravation I have for myself. "I want to find people...desperately. But I want to find them on my terms. There's no guarantee other survivors...if there are any...are good people. Taking chances is dangerous. I must start thinking things through!"

As we approach the point where the two rivers meet, we sail past another bridge crossing the mouth of the Trent River. It's a short, low swing bridge connecting the town to the huge twin bridges and secondary roads out of town. On the other side is a marina where dozens of boats litter the water like broken toys. It's doubtful any of them are still seaworthy, but it doesn't matter. They're on the other side of the swing bridge...which is closed. These boats will never access open waters again.

I drop sail, raise the keel and crank up the engine to make our approach to the Union Point docks. Three short floating piers reach out from the riverbank, two of them mangled by the storm. The third dock appears OK, so I shift the engine into neutral and glide up to the floating platform.

My luck holds and I'm able to secure the bow and stern lines to the pylons without having to get out of the boat. My fear is, if one of the floats under the dock has been ruptured, it might pitch over, or worse, sink when I step onto it. With the lines attached to the pylons, I don't have to worry about the sailboat being pulled under with the dock if it sinks.

The air is warmer now, so I shed my coat and go into the cabin. Spotting the rifle laying on the berth, I consider the pros and cons of taking it with me. If people are hiding and see I'm heavily armed, they might not make their presence known. Then again, if I do come across other survivors, they could be bad actors. I have to be able to protect myself.

The answer seems obvious. I'll keep the handgun and hide the rifle under the main berth's cushion. If something bad happens, at least I'll have a "get back" gun to fight my way to the rifle.

"Are you ready?" I ask Tonka as I pick him up by his vest's lift strap. He looks at me and licks my cheek. If the dock holds up, I'll take the vest off and toss it back into the boat.

"Here goes nothing," I say, and step onto the planks.

Chapter Thirteen

Acceptance

Tonka sniffs a small pile of salt and sand in the doorway to yet another shop, then turns to look at me with eyes that say, "There's nothing here either."

We've come across hundreds of sandpiles inside the shops, art galleries, taverns and restaurants. This is the first one we've found outside. That's because the entryway is recessed into the building. The alcove protects the small heap of silica from the wind and rain.

Tired and discouraged, I sit on a bench in front of the store. Tonka jumps up and plops down next to me.

"I don't know what they are," I say, pouring water from my bota into a cup so he can drink. "They're everywhere. We found a few back home, but nothing like here."

Tonka licks the water off his chin and gives me a "who do you think you're kidding" look. Because I do know what they are. At least I think I do. And if I'm right, the meaning of their existence is too terrible to ponder. So, I don't.

"OK, what do we do now?" I ask. The Westie answers by resting his head on my thigh, inviting me to scratch his head.

Once again, I'm forced to consider the possibilities and make decisions on my own. Just me. I'm proud of what I've done and what I've accomplished. But if I'm being honest...sometimes I wish someone else was around to tell me what to do. To not have to make all the decisions. I'm stubborn and independent, but I don't want to be an adult yet.

My fear the floating dock might sink was a big nothing burger. We stepped onto the waterfront walkway of Union Point with no problems at all. The park was deserted. No surprise there. But the scene before us was right out of Black Mirror. The pavilion was set up for a live performance. Dozens of chairs with accompanying music stands and orchestra instruments were strewn about the stage. A few lawn chairs littered the open area in front of it. There was space for hundreds more, but the wind and the flood waters had swept them away.

Dozens of cars and trucks were in the nearby parking lot, waiting for their owners to return and drive them away. That's never going to happen. These vehicles had been underwater and were ruined.

We began walking toward the center of town, passing an urban mishmash of stores, a gas station, yet another marina, and homes. We didn't go inside them at first because everything at ground level had been flooded. Mold and mildew have become a health hazard in flooded spaces. I won't put myself at risk if there's no reason.

So, you know the unexplainable feeling characters in books and movies talk about? That tingling sensation Spider-Man feels when someone is watching? I can't explain why, but I had the exact opposite experience. The farther we walked into town, the more I sensed no one was watching us. No people eyeing us from afar. No one peeping at us from behind curtains. Nobody. I gotta say, if I was going to pick a superpower...it wouldn't be the ability to sense nothingness. And what would my superhero persona be...Senseless Girl? Now that's funny.

The ground rose higher as we walked toward the center of town. After a couple of blocks, we passed buildings that hadn't flooded at all. Any damage they suffered had been caused by wind, not water.

And then we started seeing bears.

Not real bears. Lifesize fiberglass bear statues. Bears in various poses painted to look like people. There was a dentist, a shopkeeper, a pirate, and many others. Their names were puns, like Flag Bearer and Bearon DeGraffenried...one of New Bern's founders, according to the inscription. The people in this town sure love their bears and their history. It looks like it was a fun place...before The Great Vanishing. But in all our wonderings and explorations, we didn't find signs of a single living human.

Whatever happened to the people had taken place during business hours, because all the shops and stores are unlocked. It's like the employees had stepped away for a minute, expecting to come right back. Of course, when we discovered the doors were open, we began going inside.

That's when we began seeing the sandpiles. There are quite a few piles in the shops and antique stores. It looked like little kids had come from the beach and dumped their sand buckets willy-nilly on the floors. The restaurants and taverns were even worse. Sand everywhere. Nice, neat mounds of sand and salt on the floors, chairs and barstools. It reminds me of a character in the Spider-Man movies and comics...The Sandman. The supervillain who can turn himself into...wait!

My skin prickles with cold electricity as a thousand little clues bond together to create a single undeniable truth. I know what the piles of silica are, but I dare not speak it.

Knowing the truth is one thing. But saying it aloud will give it power over me, and I don't think I can handle that yet. Like a coward, I force the thought back into the dark recesses of my mind.

Tonka stirs at my side. Sensing I'm about to have some sort of post-trauma meltdown, he jumps to the sidewalk and pokes me with his nose.

"It's time to go," he says with his eyes, and I know he's right. I need to get my head straight, then decide what to do next.

The setting sun is in a sweet spot where it shines on our side of the street just before dropping behind the buildings on the other side. As we turn to leave, a glint of sunlight catches my eye. I kneel next to the small sandpile and brush away the silica to reveal a small heart-shaped locket on a fine gold chain. A lover's keepsake, perhaps? But that's not why it's important.

My mind is like pudding. The locket gives me something tangible to grasp, the way someone drowning latches onto a ring buoy. It's evidence people really lived here once and that I'm not losing my mind.

I slip the chain over my head and we return to the dock where Icebreaker is moored. After taking the seat at the stern, I stare at the locket, considering the contradiction of its existence. Tonka jumps aboard a moment later, startling me, then lies at my feet. The halyard slaps against the mast with an irregular beat as the boat bobs on the water. The sound is like a bell, clanging out an ominous warning that matches my dark musings.

With trembling fingers, I will myself to open the locket. Inside is exactly what one would expect. A small picture of a couple embraced in a kiss. Whether they are teenagers or adults, I can't tell. The details of their faces are obscured, the photo paper distorted by moisture. They could be anybody. They could be people I knew. But whoever they are, they are no longer here.

"Where on this bloody earth is everybody?" I say to Tonka. "Where have they gone?" Speaking to him as I would a person has become my lifeline to sanity. He looks at me as he always does, his dark eyes unable to convey the truths he saw during the hurricane while I had been unconscious.

"If only you could talk. If only you could tell me what you know."

I look at the picture again. Even without the details of their faces, their devotion to each other is understood. Their emotions undeniable. In my current state of mind...so long deprived of human companionship...they represent everything good with mankind. Hope, commitment, support, faith, community, family, love, perseverance. Humanity itself. And they are gone. They are *all* gone.

Despair sweeps over me. For the first time since the storm, I give serious consideration to the most terrible possibilities. For the first time since beginning my search for others, I feel helpless. Even worse, I feel hopeless. Such emotions are the opposite of everything I believe myself to be, and I have no experience coping with them.

I bury my head in my hands and cry. Sobs come in relentless waves I can't hold back. Tonka...the dear sweet Westie that allowed me into his home after my reawakening...jumps into my lap and paws at my hands. But the sobs continue until my chest hurts and I no longer have the strength to continue.

I remain on Icebreaker's deck, holding Tonka close to my heart. And though I stare across the water as the sun slips below the horizon, my eyes see nothing.

"This is not the way it's supposed to be," I whisper. "In the books and movies, the survivor of an apocalypse becomes a hero...rises above all obstacles, finds other people, and begins to rebuild. No matter how horrible their existence has become, the people in those stories have reason to live. To survive. If nothing else, there are other people in these imagined worlds, either friends or foes or both."

Tonka senses my pain and licks my face. I know it's my imagination driven by despair, but I believe he understands.

"I have everything I need to survive, to live out the rest of my life in comfort. But what's the point of having a life if there's no one to share it with? I don't even have an adversary to torment me. Nothing. This is no apocalypse. This is hell on earth...and I am the true walking dead."

CHAPTER FOURTEEN

Lost

After a restless night on Icebreaker, we awaken to an overcast sky and a light rain. To add insult to injury, my eyes itch and my throat is sore. Perfect! Nothing compliments a dark mood like gloomy weather and hay fever. It's like I'm in a movie and the scriptwriters have contrived a formulaic setting.

"This flick sucks," I say to Tonka while preparing his food. He stares at the kibbles as I dump them into a bowl. He has his priorities.

I'm not hungry, so I don't eat anything. Who cares? Tonka munches his food, then laps up some water.

My thoughts wander and I don't realize I've zoned out until he pokes me with his nose.

I take Tonka for a quick walk before we go, and notice something I'd missed before. The city still has power! Thanks to the early hour and heavy cloud cover, the streetlamps are on and inside lights shine through the windows of almost every building in view.

This fact doesn't help solve the mystery of where everybody has gone, but it is easy to explain...theoretically. Many trees along Broad Creek Road were blown down. The lines providing power to the peninsula were severed in several places. The city is closer to the power station and the trunk lines delivering electricity must be OK. And now that I'm thinking about it, the places with refrigerators didn't reek of spoiled groceries. I may want to come back for perishables later. But not too much later. They won't last forever.

What bothers me isn't that the city has power and we don't. What bothers me is the realization I hadn't noticed it right away. As lessons go, this one didn't cost me anything. But it's a stark reminder normal doesn't exist anymore. If I don't start paying attention to every detail, I won't survive. A moment of carelessness can cost me my life.

When Tonka is done leaving a parting gift for posterity...no need for poop bags now, right...we board the sailboat and shove off. Instead of using the engine, I let the boat drift with the current, using the rudder to steer clear of the huge bridge pylons. The gloom of the day and our glacier-like pace down the river pull me deeper into my dark mood.

"I guess if you have nowhere you have to be, there's no hurry to get there. Right, Tonka?"

Lying next to me on the helmsman's seat, the Westie's only response is to raise his eyes to meet mine. How a simple glance from a dog can invoke feelings of guilt and shame, I don't know. But it does.

"I know, you're right. It's not healthy to wallow in self-pity. But I can't help it. No matter how hard I try, I can't find anything positive in any of this. I...I don't know what to do."

Tonka rests his head on my thigh...a sign of acceptance he uses more and more each day...content to watch the riverbank go by as we continue our slow journey home.

My surrender to oblivion is so complete I don't realize the drizzle has become a steady rain until the terrier jumps from the seat and ducks inside the cabin. I don't know how long it's been raining. My hair and clothes are soaked. Adding to my funk, the air is so laden with moisture it's like we're drifting through a cloud. Then I realize I can't see any landmarks. I have no idea where we are!

Calm down, the voice in my head says. *Make a mental list. Tackle one problem at a time.*

"We're probably still in the channel," I say to Tonka, watching from the cabin. "The water has to flow faster in the channel, right? So, if we just keep drifting, we'll pass a channel marker. Then I can pinpoint where we are."

It's sound logic, but the fog is as thick as buttermilk. We could drift within ten feet of a marker and wouldn't see it. I wipe my nose with the back of my hand and shake off a shiver I didn't feel coming. My wet clothes are giving me a chill, so I leave the helm and go inside the cabin. After a few minutes poking around, I find a slicker and a wool stocking cap, slip them on, and return to the tiller. Despite the added clothing, an unexpected cold wave passes through me. I suppress a shiver and pull the coat tighter.

"I guess it'll take a few minutes to warm up," I say to Tonka, who's now lying in the hatchway. But warmth doesn't come, and the day grows darker.

I'm not sure how long we drift. Maybe an hour or more. I'm not in a panic, I refuse to panic. In fact, from this day forward, the word "panic" doesn't exist. Not for me. If we don't sight something soon, I'll just go to Plan C...drop anchor and wait out the rain inside the cabin.

I'm not cold anymore, but another shiver passes through me. Forget cold. Now I'm downright hot. I feel like shedding the slicker, but that wouldn't be smart.

I put my hand on my forehead and the searing truth comes to me through a new fog. One in my head. I'm sick with a fever! I have a cold or the flu or something. My body shakes and I struggle to control myself.

"This is getting serious," I say to Tonka through chattering teeth. "I feel weak. My thinking is off. We need to get home."

The muted glow of a green light dead ahead emerges from the fog and I freeze. Light means people, right? Is it a boat coming toward us? No, that can't be right. A boat's bow would have red and green lights...red for portside, green for starboard. *How do I know this? Stupid memory!*

I pull on the rudder as we come closer to make sure we don't collide. Between the fog on the water and the fog in my head, I don't realize the light is stationary until we are passing it.

"I am so stupid," I say, talking to myself, now. "It's a channel marker! The light is solar-powered. It's running on batteries."

I guide the boat so we can pass as close as possible. The number on its square placard becomes visible in the light's green glow. Then I see the figures 1-1. Yes! Marker eleven! Now I can figure out how to get us home! But I have to hurry before we lose the beacon. Time to start the engine.

When I rise to start the engine, everything around me swirls, and I lean on the tiller to keep from falling overboard. Whether I'm dizzy from fever or from sitting so long, I can't tell. But the "why" of it doesn't matter. What matters is slowing down and making my moves more deliberate. I'm not wearing a life vest and I don't have time to grab one.

After taking a minute to gather myself, I grab the starter cord handle and give it a pull. The engine sputters but doesn't start. My knees buckle, and it takes all my strength to remain upright. The possibility we're out of gas flashes through my mind and I break into a sweat.

"Sweet Mary, mother of Joseph," I plead, having no idea where the jumbled-up prayer comes from. I give the cord another yank and the engine sputters to life. "Thank you...whoever you are."

I collapse into the seat, turn the sailboat around and glide up beside the channel marker. I let the engine idle as I secure the bow line to its pylon, then shuffle inside the cabin to study the chart.

Cheese-and-rice! The chart shows we've passed the point where we should have turned up Broad Creek by several miles. It also shows a red beacon at the convergence of the creek and the river to the northwest. With the help of a protractor, I measure the distance between the markers as three-point-four nautical miles. Though I can't see the light through the fog, I know it's there. I remember passing it on the way out. If we can make it that far, we'll find the creek behind our home. Easy peasy.

The chart shows the true bearing from Marker Eleven to the one on Broad Creek is thirty-five degrees. The helm's compass will show the direction, but I have to account for the river's current...which I guesstimate to be about three miles an hour. If I'm wrong, we might run aground.

The mental gymnastics of calculating and plotting the course in my head is exhausting. Piloting isn't easy, even in good conditions. The harder I focus, the more my head hurts. If I do this wrong, we'll end up worse off than staying in place. And staying in place isn't an option. I'm growing weaker and less able to focus with each passing minute. We have to go home...now.

The wind and rain blast my face when I step out of the cabin. With trembling fingers, I retrieve the bow line, put the engine in gear, and head for the marker. If I've done my mental math correctly...given our speed and distance...we'll see the red channel light in about ten minutes.

But ten minutes pass and we see nothing but fog. Then twelve minutes. Then fifteen.

"I must have done something wrong," I say to Tonka, still watching me from the cabin. "But what? I know I plotted the beacon's location correctly. I've accounted for the current and our speed. Is the beacon not working? What have I missed?"

Fearful we might run aground, I back off the throttle to the point we almost stop. My head is pounding and the heat my body is generating inside my slicker is like a fire. The rain on my face is the only reason I haven't passed out. I'm sure of it.

"The wind! It's the wind, Tonka. I was so focused on doing the math, I hadn't noticed the wind had grown stronger. Of course it took longer to make it here, fighting the wind."

Just as the words leave my mouth, a red glow emerges from the fog and rain just a few dozen feet away. As we pass the pylon, I see the figure 2 painted on the red triangle marker confirming our position. From the chart, I remember we now need to change our heading to forty-two degrees to reach the next marker. It's not lighted, but I know it's green and only a half-mile away. From there, the entrance to our little creek is a stone's throw away.

I glance toward Tonka to say, "We're going to make it!" But the words come out as, "Ware oning ache et." I cough and strain so hard I see stars. My throat is on fire and my vocal cords feel like boa constrictors trying to crush a crocodile.

Tilting my head back, I let the rain fall into my mouth. The cool water soothes my sore throat, but does little to quench my growing thirst. I haven't had any liquids all day and I'm dehydrated. Not smart!

At last, I see the final marker come into view and I steer the cruiser up the creek. We reach the pier behind the house and I glide up to the dock. After tying off the bow and stern lines, I lift Tonka onto the dock and...gathering what little strength I have left...haul myself out of the boat.

The rain is coming down in sheets and it's almost dark. Tonka leads as I stumble forward, struggling to keep his white form in sight. The few minutes it takes to reach the end of the pier seem like hours, but we finally pass the Catalina leaning against the back steps and enter the house through the center stairwell.

Somehow sensing I have only moments before collapsing, I will myself to chug down a bottle of water, take off my wet clothes, and pull on a heavy robe. A wave of fatigue hits me, but I fight my way through it and crawl under the sheets of the master bed. Though having washed and changed the bedding days ago, I hadn't slept in it yet. A last trespass of the home's sanctity I'd been unwilling to commit. Now, I no longer cared. The last thing I'm aware of before I pass out is Tonka jumping onto the bed and lying next to me. Then a veil of black.

CHAPTER FIFTEEN

Fever

Time becomes an immeasurable abstract. No beginning, no end. No future, no past. Only moments of the present in which I am awake, disoriented and without purpose. And then I lapse into another fevered sleep.

There are moments when I'm vaguely aware of taking a shower or preparing soup or feeding Tonka. Actions that begin but have no conclusion. I can never recall drying off or eating the food or taking the Westie outside. Yet, I know I did. At least I think I did. I must have.

On the second day...or maybe the third...I awake to darkness. I try to open my mouth, but my lips refuse to part. My skin is like a sponge left too long in the desert sun. The heat my body generates and the sheet I'm under form an unbearable sauna.

I kick off the sheet and the cold air shocks me the same way plunging into ice water would. Tonka grunts his annoyance at having been disturbed. I've not made a fire in the woodstove for days and the outside temperature has plummeted since we've been home. It's no wonder the Westie is curled up beside me.

My brain is functioning at the speed of molasses on a winter's day. I need to counter the fever, but how? I'm standing in the middle of the great room wearing no clothes, heat radiating from my body. I'm not sure why I've come here. Then I see the refrigerator in the kitchen and remember.

"Water..." I say through parched lips. "Must have water."

Oblivious to everything around me, I open the refrigerator, grab a bottle of overpriced designer water, unscrew the cap, and drink the eleven-point-five ounces of cold, clear liquid goodness from heaven in a series of gulps I can't stop until I've downed the entire contents. The H2O flows down my esophagus and into my stomach where, I swear, I can feel my insides absorbing the life-sustaining liquid, then dispersing it to my bone-dry cells. Relief is immediate, but not complete.

I open another water bottle and drink half its contents before I'm forced to stop to let my stomach catch up. Too much liquid can be as bad as not drinking enough. I press the cold plastic container against my forehead, relishing its relief. As I bring my hand down, a flicker of light catches my eye. I look through the wall of glass dividing the great room and back porch and stare into the dark.

Nothing. Was it my imagination?

I don't trust my senses, so I step out onto the porch to take a better look and realize my stupidity. The cold in the house is nothing compared to the icy air outside...and me with no clothes on! Though my body is still ablaze with fever, it isn't hot enough to counter the arctic air I've stepped into. This won't do! This won't do at all!

I stumble over the threshold because I'm moving fast and my balance is off, but I make it inside. And just like that, I'm not cold anymore. The bonfire inside my body rages on. The reprieve granted by the outside cold was temporary.

"I'm sick," I say to Tonka, who has come into the great room to see what all the commotion is about. "I am so very sick."

But the mystery of the light remains. I have to know what it is! So I find the heavy robe and pull it on. Still barefoot, I step out on the porch again with Tonka on my heels. And there it is!

"Look!" I whisper, not believing my eyes. "It's a fire! On the other side of Broad Creek. The one between our creek and the river. For real!"

Rejuvenated by the adrenaline coursing through my veins, I spin around to grab my binoculars inside the house. The sudden movement is too much. I crash to the porch floor.

Awareness rushes back with a WHOOSH. Tonka is licking my face and I realize I'm still on the porch in the freezing cold. I don't know how long I've been out. I don't think it was long. It's still dark.

Gathering my strength, I pick myself up and go to the bedroom. Each motion I make while dressing is pure agony and my head is throbbing to the beat of Queen's "We Will Rock You!" But I have to cross Broad Creek to see what...or who...started the fire. Waiting until tomorrow may be too late.

My body moves on autopilot as I dump food into Tonka's bowl and top off his water. I don't know how long this will take. And given my condition, I'm not sure I'll make it back. But I have a plan.

"I'm sorry," I say to my little buddy as I pull on my heavy coat, "but you can't go this time. It's dark and I'm too weak to save you if something happens. You'll be OK. I'm leaving the door downstairs cracked open so you can go outside if...if anything happens to me."

OK, it's not a brilliant plan, but it has to be this way. If I weren't so weak, it would be different. If anything happens to me, he'll be better off here. And if the fire is some kind of trap, I doubt I can protect either of us.

I kneel to the floor in front of him and, grasping his flews with both hands, plant a kiss on the sweet spot between his eyes.

"I love you, Tonka. I'll be back for you. Trust me on this. As long as I have breath, I'll come back. You're the only friend I have, and I'll never abandon you."

He knows I'm leaving him. I can see it in his eyes and it's breaking my heart. But it's the right thing to do. I hope.

Not daring to look back, I grab a flashlight, step out the front door, and close it behind me. But there's one more thing to do before leaving. As quietly as possible, I open the door to the stairwell under the house and place a brick in the jamb so it can't close. If I don't make it back, Tonka can go outside and try to make it on his own. Like I said, it's not a great plan.

The walk down the long, wet pier in the darkness is precarious. It's not raining, but the clouds are heavy and ready to release their moisture at any moment. At least there's no wind. Given my weak condition, that's a big deal. Anything beyond a breeze would blow me off the pier and into the marsh.

Somehow, while holding the flashlight under my arm, I untie the mooring lines and start the engine. Thanks to the recent rain, the water is high. But I force myself to go slow so I don't run aground on the mud banks. As I turn the boat around to head out, I see a small white form emerge from the darkness to stand on the dock's edge.

"Tonka!" I yell. "Go back! Go back to the house! You can't come with me!"

Instead of obeying, he sits on his haunches and stares at me as I'm pulling away. He makes such a pitiful sight, I almost stop. I'm sure he thinks I'm abandoning him. But I can't stop. I can't put him in danger. I won't!

"I'll be back Tonka!" I yell, but I don't think he can hear me over the engine. And then in a whisper, "I love you, Tonka. I'll be back, I swear it."

With tears running down my cheeks, I gun the engine and head toward the open water. When I reach Broad Creek, I peer into the darkness and spot the fire compelling me to make what may be the dumbest decision of my life. I'm growing weaker with each passing minute. Only adrenaline and hope keep me going. I have to know what's there.

Minutes later, I'm closing in on the far bank where the fire still burns. It's a controlled fire, contained in a fire pit behind someone's home. It's the type of stone pit families gather around to roast marshmallows and tell ghost stories. On the short, stone-wall bench surrounding the patio, silhouetted by the fire, sits what looks to be a man with his back turned toward me. If he hears me approaching the dock, he doesn't show it.

His lack of a reaction unnerves me, but I've come too far to stop now. With shaking hands, I secure the bow line to a cleat and walk down the short pier. My legs are rubber, like in one of those bad dreams where you desperately try to run from something but move in slow motion.

The effort to walk the last few feet saps all my strength. Sweat flows from my pores, soaking the clothes under my heavy coat. I'm close enough to touch the man now. Still, he doesn't turn.

"Hello, Turpi," he says. "I've been waiting for you. Come, sit by the fire. I don't have much time."

Any other time, I would turn and run away. But my weird sixth sense tells me not to. It says everything is OK. Or maybe I'm so sick I no longer care. I haven't seen or heard a human being in weeks. There's no way I'm leaving.

I will my heavy legs to step over the wall to sit across from the man. Firelight dances across his face. I'm barely able to breathe. He's middle-aged with a well-groomed, graying beard. The bone structure not concealed by facial hair is well-defined, covered by fair skin creased by lines of knowledge and wisdom. The color of both his hair and his eyes are dark, though their exact pigments are impossible to distinguish by firelight. But I don't need to see the color of his eyes to tell they look at me with kindness and...pride?

"Is Turpi my name?" I ask. It seems a good place to start.

The man smiles with sad eyes, like he's remembering a bittersweet song.

"It's your nickname," he says. "It's the name I gave you on your fifth birthday, the night you discovered a leatherback laying eggs on the beach during my research sabbatical on Portsmouth Island. You were terribly upset because the turtle was crying. You thought it had been injured. I explained, sea turtles cry to maintain the correct balance of salt in their bodies and to wash sand from their eyes. That they do it all the time, but we can't see it until they come ashore to lay their eggs.

"You didn't believe me until the turtle moved off the nest and you saw the eggs as she covered them with sand. And then you did the most amazing thing. You went to the front of this beautiful sea creature and began stroking her enormous head to comfort her. You were fearless. Do you remember what you said?"

I shake my head, not sure I believe him.

"As you rubbed the turtle's head, you whispered, 'I know the real reason you cry, Mrs. Turtle. You cry because you know many of your eggs will be eaten by raccoons and foxes before they hatch. And many of those that do hatch will be eaten by birds and crabs as they crawl to the sea. And many of the ones that reach the ocean will be eaten by fish.' And when I asked why you believed such things, do you remember what you said?"

I say nothing because I don't recall any of it. And the fear I may never remember any of my past life has become a steel band around my chest, squeezing the air from my lungs.

"You said, 'Because she told me so, just now. Science doesn't know everything, daddy. Science can measure the universe, but it can't measure love.'"

I stare into the fire, mulling over his words, trying to pull the scene he described from my lost memories...but it won't come. Yet, I feel a connection to the story vibrating through my body the way energy makes the wires on an electric fence hum. Like electricity, I can't see it, but I know it's real.

"So, you're my father?" I ask.

He gazes into the fire just as I had done moments before, considering his reply. Then he turns and looks into my eyes.

"You have always been a very special person, Turpi. The voyage you began a year ago was the most noble quest ever undertaken by a girl your age. Though the world has changed, your quest isn't over. It simply means the goals have changed. The world needs you. Humanity needs you. I know you won't let us down."

The fire pops, throwing sparks into the air, startling me. As if on cue, the rain begins. Not a downpour, but a steady rain that will soon douse the fire.

"Why me?" I ask. But he's gone. Covering my eyes to block the firelight, I stare into the darkness to see where he has gone. There's movement along the tree line surrounding the house and I think I see him disappear into the woods...but I can't be sure.

"Wait!" I yell. "You didn't tell me my name! What is my real name?"

But there is no reply.

CHAPTER SIXTEEN

Visions

Pungent odors of organic soil and dank decay fill my nostrils when I awake. I struggle to open my heavy eyelids, but what I see makes no sense. It's like the surface of the moon, only black. I lift my head and the pounding in my temples returns with a vengeance. One of those Gaia-worshipping drum circles has taken up residence behind my eyeballs. An attempt to swallow makes me gag, as there is no moisture in my throat.

Water. I need water. It's been hours since I drank the bottled water back home. Water will stop the pounding in my head and revitalize my dried-out organs.

Not until I try to stand do I realize I was lying face down in the dirt next to the patio all night. I must have passed out after my father left. But...was he my father? I play the scene back in the theater of my mind, but don't recall him ever saying he was. Was what I saw real or a fever-induced hallucination?

My muscles shake with weakness as I pull myself up to sit on the stone bench surrounding the patio. Was it last night? How long have I been lying here? I have no way of knowing. There is no smoke coming from the fire pit. Had the rain doused the fire? Had there ever been a fire?

A quick look around reveals no evidence the mystery man was ever here, not even footprints. I scan the wood line, hoping to see a path he may have taken when he left. No joy.

I start to stand, but a movement in the woods catches my eye. An ice-cold jolt of adrenalin shoots through my veins as a red wolf steps into the yard and I freeze. A wave of fear cascades on top of the adrenaline because I've lost track of where I left Tonka! Where's Tonka? And then I remember I forced him to stay home.

OK, Ivy Moon, think before acting!

I rack my brain for anything that might help and recall the article I read on the computer about red wolves. That they were released into the wild northeast of here. The Neuse River is more than a hundred miles from their sanctuary, but here he is, staring right at me. I guess with all the people gone, the wolves no longer fear roaming the land.

I also remember, the worst thing to do is to run...just like with big dogs. So, I try to make myself look as large as possible while remaining stone-still. I know it sounds dumb, but that's what you're supposed to do.

We stare at each other like two gunfighters in one of those old wild west movies...only I don't have any weapons. I was so out of it when I left the house, I forgot to bring mine. And just like last time...with the bear...I think I'm gonna wet my pants. I can't muster up enough moisture to spit, yet I'm going to wet myself? What is it with me?

As we continue staring at each other, I notice gray fur on the wolf's snout. This means he has some age on him...which is weird...because the relocated wolves can't be very old. Even weirder, I get a creepy feeling I've seen him before. Who knows, maybe I have. I have no idea what kind or how many animals I've seen in my life. The selective memory thing, you know.

The longer our eyes remain locked, the more I'm drawn into his thoughts. My initial fear is replaced with cautious trust and my imagination wanders. I'm overcome with images of the world as it is becoming. With no people to pave the roads and mow the grass, the wild things will soon take over and earth will return to the way it was before mankind.

Wolves and bears are only the beginning. Populations of small animals like squirrels, rabbits, otters and beavers will explode, creating a bounty for predators like wolves, wild dogs, bobcats and feral house cats. Predators will become more numerous...and more of a threat.

I see populations of doves, ducks and geese growing so large they blank out the sun. Fish become so abundant it will be possible to scoop them out of the water with a hand net. Nature will find a balance, but there will be extreme population swings until then. And I wonder, what chance does a teenage girl and a small dog have in such a dangerous future?

Rain begins falling on my face. I blink and I see the wolf is sitting now, still staring at me, not posing a threat. Had he somehow triggered such vivid visions? My head is pounding from the overload of imaginings and the lack of water. It's time to leave.

Before rising from the stone bench, I break the wolf's gaze long enough to survey the path to the pier. It will take all my strength to make it back to the boat, and I don't want to take a chance on tripping over a root or stumbling. The red wolf watches me with sad, knowing eyes. He isn't a threat...he is a messenger.

Untying the bow line, I hop into the sailboat, push away from the pier, and start the engine. Wind and rain blow across my face as I motor across water, which is good. The cold keeps me from passing out. The sun is at my back, a dull yellow orb muted by dark clouds. At least I know it's morning. But which morning?

Halfway back to the narrow creek, my bladder knots up and I groan in agony. I shift the engine to neutral and leave the stern long enough to use the head...but little comes out. How could I have been dying to use the bathroom and yet be so dehydrated? A girl's body can be a weird thing.

I take a moment to grab a couple of water bottles from the boat's mini fridge to rehydrate, then take my seat at the rudder. It's not much, but the cramps subside and I shift the engine into gear. At last, the pier comes into view as I navigate around the last bend in our shallow creek and I see something white on the dock.

"Tonka!" I yell, but the small mound of fur doesn't stir.

I cut off the engine at the last second and the sailboat crashes broadside into the dock's supporting pylons. The cruiser is damaged, but I don't care. I wrap the bow line around a cleat, drop to my knees and lift the Westie to my chest. He's shivering, but alive. He's been on the dock exposed to the cold and rain for as long as I've been gone...however long that's been.

My heart shattered by guilt, I tuck Tonka inside my coat and carry him inside the house as fast as my weak legs will allow. Tears stream down my face as I wrap the terrier in a towel and lay him in his doggy bed next to the woodstove. My numb fingers keep dropping the lighter as I try to ignite a pile of kindling in the firebox until...finally...a small flame sputters to life and grows. After piling on logs as fast as the expanding fire will allow, I close the stove's glass door and open the intake vent to create the hottest blaze possible.

But I'm not finished yet. I go to the kitchen, fill Tonka's bowl with fresh water, and sit next to him. I dip my hand in the bowl and I dribble water onto his lips. He licks the moisture from my fingers, then sits up. When he has his fill, he tries to lick my face to say thank you. And that's when the dam breaks. With tears flowing from my eyes, I pull him onto my lap and stroke his head.

"Tonka," I whisper. "I will never leave you again. Never. I swear."

I hug him for a moment, then place him back on the bed under the towel. Unable to deny my own needs any longer, I go to the fridge long enough to drink as much water as I can hold and return to the great room. Exhausted, I lie down in front of the woodstove and pull Tonka, still in his bed, up against my body. Together, we sleep the sleep of the dead.

Frankly, My Dear

Time is lost to me. I don't know how long we sleep. As it had before, the fever turns hours and days into episodes of shadow and light. As best as I can tell by looking at the computer's date stamp, I was sick for an entire week. But I hadn't made note of what day it was when the fever started, so I can't be sure. The truth is, it doesn't matter.

The better I feel, the greater my appetite grows. I lost a lot of weight during my illness and I need to regain my strength. There's lots of work to do. Wash clothes and linens, cut wood for the stove, repair the damage I did to the sailboat...which wasn't bad, thank goodness. I also have to scavenge. We are running low on food and I need to resupply.

I hate such mundane tasks, but this is different. My brain is mush and I don't want to think, to plan, to dwell. I exist in the moment, trying to stay busy, trying not to think about my loneliness. Loneliness leads to hopelessness. Hopelessness turns to pity. I will *not* pity myself. Besides, Tonka who is always by my side, so I will never be alone while he is around. He is my salvation.

We have entered the teeth of winter and I'm glad to have plenty of firewood. I regulate the wood stove so it burns long and slow and only when we need it. My closet is every house in the world, and it contains an endless supply of sweaters, sweatshirts, and thick flannel shirts I wear in the house. When we venture outside, I have an endless collection of down coats, vests and insulated leather jackets from which to choose.

And boots! I have tons of boots! Best of all, I found *the* most excellent pair of all-leather moccasins that reach just below my knees. They fit perfectly and I love how they look with my jeans tucked in...so I wear them most of the time. I also have hiking boots, steel-toed boots, ankle boots, calf-high boots, thigh-high boots, waterproof boots and even insulated wading boots...if I want them. I mean, I don't have all of them here, but I know where they are. It's all on my inventory sheet.

I also have dog clothes Tonka can wear. A sweater and a rain slicker. They are *too* cute, and he doesn't complain when he needs to wear them. It's like he remembers almost dying of overexposure on the dock and understands their purpose. I also found a strange little costume for a dog his size. If I put it on him, he'd look like a pilgrim carrying a musket. But I would never force him to wear such a ridiculous thing. He has his dignity.

The winter clothes are more than niceties, as we are discovering.

"According to the information I have on the computer file about this part of North Carolina, the winters are mild," I say to Tonka as we stand on the back porch, watching huge wet flakes fall. "But it does snow sometimes. Have you ever seen it snow before?"

He continues staring out over the backyard and the marsh, fascinated by the gentle storm of white. Challenger's deck is already covered, and the ground is disappearing as well.

"This article also says global warming will make it so warm, children ten years from now won't know what snow is. But the article is twenty years old. I wonder why the prediction never came true?"

Tonka scratches at the screen door to go out. Of course, we can't go that way because of the sailboat, so we use the middle stairway. Before leaving the open area under the house, we pause to look and listen. It's amazing to live in a world so quiet we can hear snow falling on the grass. The thought makes me smile. Living in the apocalypse isn't all bad. And who doesn't like snow!

My rubber boots crunch over the snow covering the pier as we walk toward the creek. Tired of trying to bite the flakes, Tonka takes off toward the dock. I keep my pace slow as the planks are slippery and I don't want to take a header into the marsh mud.

"Slow down!" I yell, but he keeps going until he reaches the dock. In an instant, he turns tail and runs back toward me, coming to a Scooby-Doo style sliding stop at my feet. Something scared him! I can't imagine what it might be, but I'm not worried. I never leave the house anymore without my sidearm.

I unholster my handgun as we approach the dock, listening for anything out of place. And then I hear...something really weird. Water splashing and flapping noises. Then...crunch, crunch!

Whatever it is, it's on the other side of the sailboat and I can't see it. Now, my steps are more like ice skating than walking. Moving in stealth mode, I angle myself to see the water on the other side of the boat. Only, it's not water. It's ice. It's so cold, the brackish creek water has frozen over. So, what's making the noise?

A dark and shiny form erupts from the middle of the creek where the ice is still forming. A half-beat behind it, a bigger, darker animal propels itself onto the ice sheet, sliding up to what I now realize is a mullet. The otter throws the fish up into the air by its tail and catches it in his mouth, headfirst.

Crunch. Crunch. Crunch. The otter consumes the fish in three bites, then slides back through the hole in the ice. A moment later, another otter chases a fish through the opening and repeats the unappetizing process. Tonka stares, not sure what to make of it all.

"They're very clever," I say, "but man, sometimes nature is pretty disgusting to watch."

"Roo, roo, roo!" Tonka barks, feeling braver. I can't help but laugh.

"That has got to be the silliest bark a dog ever had. You know, you kinda sound like a cartoon character."

Instead of listening to me, he's walking around the dock with his chest puffed out, acting like he's done something big. I love this dog.

On the way back to the house, I scoop up some snow, roll it into a ball, and toss it to Tonka. When he tries to catch it, it explodes in his mouth. He looks at snow-ball clumps scattered on the planks and then looks at me like, "What the heck?"

Again I laugh, and I realize it's been a long time since I've smiled or had this much fun. It's a great day.

When we get back to the house, I remove our wet garments and hang them around the great room to dry. I grab a few logs from the pile by the back door and throw them onto the fire, but this time I leave the door to the woodstove open so we can enjoy looking into the open flames.

"I'm starving," I say, and Tonka's ears perk up. "It's time to eat...and I know exactly what I want!"

A few seconds of poking around in the freezer and...woot! Hotdogs! When they've thawed enough to stick on wire clothes hangers, I roast them over the open flames. Tonka loves that. Yeah, yeah, I know. Hot dogs are not the best food for dogs to eat, but these are kosher and it's not like I do it every day. So sue me non-existent PETA lawyers.

With our stomachs full, we sit in front of the woodstove, staring into the flames. Pressing concerns about the future try to worm their way into my tranquility...but I force them back. Today is a holiday of sorts...and I'm taking full advantage of it. After all, tomorrow is another day...right Scarlett?

CHAPTER EIGHTEEN

Beaufort

For five days in a row, I sit on the back porch a while to watch the whitetail deer feeding on the lawn. It's early April, and though fawns aren't usually born until May and June, I can count at least a dozen spotted newborns. It appears every doe capable of procreating, has.

The future I saw in my wolf-vision is coming true. Whitetails giving birth early instinctively know many more fawns are coming. Their fawns, having already been born, will have an advantage over those that follow. They will be stronger than the newborns, better able to forage. Better able to survive predators. It's a strategy I see other species adopting and a phenomenon probably happening across the planet. The population explosion among wild animals is a giant exclamation point to the notion that haunts my waking hours...the age of man is over.

Tonka sits on my lap, watching the deer with unblinking eyes, not making a sound. He has become as used to seeing them as I have. He's learned barking at them serves no purpose. They only move a few feet away and continue feeding. Their numbers are so great, they have no fear of barking dogs.

Today is special. The air is warm and clear, and it's been a long time since we've gone on an outing. And today, we try something new. We've taken the boat out several times...to fish, to explore New Bern, to make supply runs. I've discovered we can dock the boat at the other end of the twin bridges in a little town named Bridgeton. From there, it's just a two-mile trip to a grocery store.

The store provides an almost endless supply of food, but there are drawbacks. It stinks to high heaven because of all the rotting vegetables and meat. I have to use one of those respirators spray painters wear to go inside. The smell has become more tolerable since I began leaving the doors open. Although animals have taken all the rotten meat, things like eggs and melons still stink so bad they can gag a maggot...as they used to say.

Anyway, I found keys to a car at the store's service desk, then located the sweet little SUV in the parking lot they go with. Now, when I make a supply run, I sail the boat to Bridgeton, hop in the car where I leave it near the water, and drive to the grocery store. I put food in the car, drive it back to the bridge, and then load up the boat. Easy peasy, lemon squeezy.

The best part is, I have a car and access to the open road. As long as I have gas, I can go anywhere. Of course, gas is pretty much everywhere because I have a siphon. But what's the point? I've spent hours on the sailboat's VHF radio and nothing. Other than a storm warning repeating itself for six months, there's no radio traffic at all. If I ever find evidence of people out there…anywhere…I'll jump in the SUV and go. But until that happens, I'm not straying far from the water.

As I said, today is special. We're taking a trip to the coast. Spring weather is unpredictable and I should probably wait a few more weeks, but I can't stand it. I need to do something different. Plus, there's an invisible force drawing me to the ocean. It's because of who I am. You know? My sailing skills and my first memory of waking up on the boat after the storm.

I can't explain it, but my heart tells me if I go exploring, I'm better off sailing the waterways than driving across land. There's no doubt about it. I'm a water person and that's all there is to it.

"OK, Tonka. It's time to go. You ready?"

The Westie jumps from my lap and goes to the middle stairway door, the quickest way to the dock. He's a really smart dog.

The deer watch our odd little parade with curiosity as we head out to the pier. Tonka leads the way and I follow, pulling a garden wagon filled with extra clothes behind me. It's kind of crazy. I mean, if I need meat, it's right there. I doubt I'll ever have to kill a deer for food...I'm just saying. Now chicken, I won't lie. I could go for a chicken sandwich or some lemon butter chicken thighs. And eggs! OMG! I'd die for some scrambled cheese eggs. Real cheese. Not goop from a squeeze can.

"We need some goats and chickens," I say to Tonka, leading the way. "Think about it. We could make almost anything if we had goats and chickens. I'm talking pancakes, waffles, omelets, cake, biscuits and...loaf bread! Mmmm.... Sourdough fried egg sandwiches with a slice of goat cheese! Doesn't that sound awesome?"

Tonka looks back at me, wondering why I sound so excited, but keeps walking.

"And syrup! There's plenty of syrup at the grocery store and tons of flour. We could make stacks of pancakes and top them with goat-milk butter and maple syrup!"

My mouth is watering and the granola bar I had for breakfast feels like a rock sitting in my stomach. I hadn't thought about it until now, but I need to plan for self-sustainability. I'll never run out of canned food, but I need fresh vegetables and dairy products, too. The next time we go to town, I'll look for seeds. It's almost planting season.

After storing the extra clothes in the cabin, I lift Tonka into Icebreaker and we head out. I've stocked her with enough food and water to last several days, filled up the gas tank and added an extra five-gallon can for back-up. We'll never be worried about running out of gas in the middle of nowhere. I've also laid out three navigation charts I'm most likely to need and plotted a course to a coastal town named Beaufort.

"All things considered, this should be an easy trip," I say to Tonka as we enter the river. "The first leg is only fifteen miles down the Neuse to a place named Adam's Creek. It starts off as a natural waterway, then becomes a manmade channel that cuts through another fifteen miles of land to Beaufort. It's part of the ICW, which stands for Intracoastal Waterway."

Tonka gives me a "I don't know what that means and don't care," look, and I laugh.

"Yeah, I know, if you can't eat it or chase it...who cares, right?"

I had been waiting for a good-weather day to attempt this journey and it looks like I've picked a great one. The sky is clear, and the air feels more like June than April. The water is still cold, of course. It will take weeks before the water temperature catches up to the air temperature, but I don't plan to go swimming, anyway.

"Best of all, there's only a light breeze," I say to Tonka, finishing my thoughts out loud. "I'll use the mainsail as long as the breeze is behind us, but the current will carry us to Adam's Creek, regardless.

We'll use the outboard if there's no wind on the ICW. Once we're at the other end of the canal, it's just a couple of miles to Beaufort."

As we enter the open water of the Neuse, I raise sail and settle back into the seat, hand on the tiller. The breeze is behind us and the sun shines on my face. As always, I keep an eye out for signs of people, but I long ago accepted the probability I won't. I'm not giving up, just being realistic.

Until today, we've only been a couple of miles downstream. Houses line the New Bern side of the river, but there's little on our side. The farther we go, the less development there is. After an uneventful hour of sailing, the river narrows and I see a large building off the starboard side.

I check the chart and see it's part of a military facility named Cherry Point, an air station for Marine Corps aircraft. I had seen it on maps and charts before, but hadn't given it much thought. Now that we're seeing it for real, I think about it in a whole different light.

"You know, Tonka, this place must have all kinds of electronics and communication equipment. It may even have its own power source to run that equipment. I bet it has a lot of survival food and gear, too. One day soon, we need to check this place out."

I look down and see the Westie next to my feet, asleep.

"Do you have any idea how lucky you are?" I ask, though I know he's not listening. But it's me who's the lucky one. Much to my credit, I know it.

After Cherry Point, we pass a dock used by ferries to carry vehicles to the other side of the river. As we sail by the terminal, I see a ferryboat loaded with cars and trucks, where they will spend the rest of eternity waiting to cross the river. It's another reminder of how strange the Great Vanishing is and how bizarre my life has become.

A few minutes later, we enter Adam's Creek. The good news is, the ICW was built wide and makes for easy boating. The bad news is, the waterway cuts through a forest and the trees block the breeze. With no wind, I'm forced to drop sail, start the engine and continue on toward the coast at a slow pace.

Houses along the banks overlook the water, silent sentinels that once surveyed the passing boats and ships. Now they are monuments to a bygone era. It's hard to believe, but one day these homes will disappear like the people who once lived in them.

"OK, enough of this morbid stuff," I say to Tonka. "It's a beautiful day and the entire planet belongs to us. Let's make the most of it!"

I put the engine in neutral and go to the cabin to retrieve an MP3 player and a Bluetooth speaker I commandeered from a house in our neighborhood. I don't know who owned the player, but they put together a great selection of tunes...everything from Ariana Grande to Warren Zevon. No, I had never heard of Warren Zevon before finding the player, but Tonka and I both love his song Werewolves of London. Hehehehehe...

Now, however, I'm in the mood to hear something epic to match our journey. So, I search for Dire Straits, call up "Sultans of Swing," and crank the speaker up to ten! If anybody's out there, they're going to hear us coming...and we'll be coming in style.

And on we go, legendary guitar riffs echoing off the houses along the canal like I'm the only person in the world...which I am...so who cares? But it makes me feel good, and I need more of that.

We reach the end of the canal and the water opens up into a cross between a wide river and an open sound. I turn down the music...which is now playing "Havana" by Camila Cabello...and consult the chart to make sure I'm following the channel markers correctly. Sweet! We're only a couple of miles away from our destination.

Technically, Beaufort isn't on the ocean. It sits on the mainland and there are three islands staggered between it and the Atlantic. It makes sense people settled here back in the colonial days because it's a well-protected harbor.

The town comes into view as we pilot around a bend in the channel and motor parallel to its main street on the waterfront. Playing songs by Camila is rockin' my inner Latina, so I find "Whenever–Wherever" by Shakira and crank up the speaker again.

My thinking regarding the best way to enter a new place has changed since the first trip to New Bern. Back then, I kept a low profile, in case any survivors I found were bad guys. Now, I make all the noise as I can. If the people who hear me turn out to be thugs, so be it. At this point, I don't care. I'll accept warm human beings in any form they come. If they're bad guys, I'll deal with them appropriately.

So, playing music loud makes sense. If there's anyone here, they'll hear my tunes and we'll find each other. Without it, we could be within a block of each other and never know. Besides, it's like I have a soundtrack for my own personal movie. How cool is that?

I'm scanning the streets and shops as we pass, but something on an island to our starboard catches Tonka's attention and he barks. Standing fetlock deep in the water are a dozen wild horses. I hadn't expected that. They watch us with a curious eye but show no fear. They're used to seeing people, even if it's been a while.

After reaching the end of the business area, I turn the boat around and make a second pass, music still blaring. Nothing. No survivors waving hysterically. No welcoming band. Not even a parade led by seventy-six trombones. Yes, I've actually seen The Music Man. *And I suddenly remember I like musicals. My stupid selective memory strikes again.* All things considered, I wish there *was* trouble in River City. At least it would mean there are people.

The marina here is more damaged than the ones in New Bern. Probably because it's closer to the ocean where the storm came ashore. There are dozens of sunken boats and many more piled on top of each other like giant toys. On the upside, finding a place to dock is no problem at all.

"Beaufort must have been a neat town," I say to Tonka as we walk along the main street. "A bit touristy, but it has some cool stores and shops. There's a hotel over there overlooking the water. We can stay there tonight if you want."

A dust devil crosses the street in front of us with a piece of paper caught in its vortex. The wind is picking up and I'm pretty sure the temperature is dropping. If it's going to turn cold, I'd much rather stay on land than in the boat on the water.

We wander around downtown for about an hour, but find no signs of people. We only go inside one shop, a store with merchandise and novelties for pets. I find a great new collar for Tonka. It's black and has little skulls and crossbones stitched into it. I also stock up on specialty dog food and treats...the healthy kind. At least, the packaging says it's healthy.

We also come across several historical markers, one of which gives me a new perspective about the town. The inscription says Beaufort was invaded by Spanish pirates in 1747, which explains why there's so much pirate stuff in the shops. Who doesn't love a good pirate story?

On the way back to the waterfront, we pass a maritime museum featuring ongoing boat-building projects. Two boats in progress...a sailboat and a quarter boat...are supported by scaffolding designed to be removed when ready to launch. It's sad to know they will never be completed. They are beautiful reconstructions of a by-gone era. But then, in my new world, every man-made thing in existence is from a by-gone era. As am I.

Returning to a hotel on the waterfront, I lift some keys from behind the front desk and find a room on the upper level which shows no sign of being occupied before the Great Vanishing. But there's still some daylight left, and it's too early to go to bed. Taking advantage of a landscaped natural area next to the hotel, I gather paper and wood to build a fire. The breeze coming off the water makes starting it difficult, but I use a plastic sandwich board sign to create a windbreak and soon have a good fire burning. As the flames grow, I make a mental note to douse the fire when we're done. There may not be any people left for it to matter, but I'd rather not burn the whole town down.

In true campfire fashion, I open a can of Vienna sausages and skewer them with wire clothes hangers to heat over the coals. Tonka lies down next to me, keeping an eye on the meat to make sure I cook it right. I also open a pack of saltine crackers to go with the sausages, but we're both starving, so we eat them right away.

As the sun sets, the temperature drops along with it, but it's not just because of nightfall. Clouds are moving in from the northeast and the storm I predicted will arrive during the night. I glance across the water to the island, but don't see any horses. I guess they have moved to the interior where there's better shelter. No doubt about it, there's a storm coming.

"Eat up," I say to Tonka, giving him a sausage. "I doubt it will be possible to make a fire in the morning, so we'll be eating light. We need to load up calories for the return home."

When we finish, I stare into the fire, thinking about what I've accomplished by coming here. Not much. I've confirmed my sailing and navigation skills are as good as I thought, and we've confirmed there aren't any people here.

"I guess the one good thing to take away from this trip is knowing we can take longer and farther trips," I say to Tonka. We've both eaten a whole can of sausages and a pack of crackers, so we're full. "I may not be the last person on earth, but if there are others out there, I doubt we'll find them by staying in one place. When we get back home, I'll create a methodical way to explore places farther and farther away. How does that sound?"

A sudden gust of wind blows sparks from the fire and we jump back to avoid being singed. I douse the fire and, with the help of a flashlight from our boat, we make our way back to the hotel room.

All I can say is…it was a real day. And it was a good day. But it wasn't a really good day.

CHAPTER NINETEEN

Kayaker

The morning greets us with a cold vengeance. Not freezing, but the air is pushed by a nor'easter. The wind chill is brutal. It's going to be an uncomfortable trip home.

I make a note on my inventory log about the hotel and the room in case we ever return. I even make the bed because...that's what you're supposed to do. Proper etiquette should always be maintained, even in an apocalypse.

After topping off Icebreaker's tank, we sail away from Beaufort with my speaker blasting out one last song..."Goodbye to You" by Patty Smyth and Scandal.

It's always good to have extra fuel, just in case. But today we don't need the engine. The wind is blowing at a robust twenty-five to thirty knots, so we are making good time.

Tonka is wearing his coat even though he's sitting in the doorway to the cabin out of the wind. I don't blame him. I'm bundled up in a heavy slicker, stocking cap, and gloves. We're both wearing our motorcycle goggles because the icy wind is murder on our eyes. These things are *so* handy.

We're making such good time, it takes only minutes to reach the ICW. The trees along the canal block some of the wind, but they can't stop the brunt of a nor'easter. At least there's no need to use the engine. We continue on under sail.

It takes half the time to traverse the canal as it did yesterday. I do some quick mental calculations and estimate we'll make it home by lunchtime. But when we come to the mouth of Adam's Creek and see the Neuse, I'm forced to reevaluate. The river is choppy and blanketed with white caps galore. The wave troughs are formidable. I can go fast and take a beating, or slow down and make it easier on us.

Hmmm... What would Jordan Turpin do?

"This is going to be a blast," I say, ducking into the cabin. While the boat is drifting, I pull on my life vest and strap Tonka into his. "OK, my little friend! Let's see what this cruiser can do in a real blow!"

Though he doesn't know what's going on, Tonka follows me to the stern, anyway. This dog has game! I clip a tether to his vest and reach for the jack line to raise the sail...but stop. I just can't help myself. I pull up an MP3 track of Lindsey Stirling's "Roundtable Rival" and turn the speaker level to ten. My heart is beating about a hundred-and-fifty miles an hour as I raise the sail. Icebreaker shoots into the river and explodes through the first swell like a cannonball, drenching us with spray.

"Yeeeee...haiiiiii!!!" I yell above the wind and music, a big smile pasted across my face. I should be shivering from the cold, but I don't even feel it now. I'm riding a wave of adrenaline and loving it.

The tiller strains in my hand like a wild beast and I fear the wind will shred the sail. Tough cookies! It's no time to be a wuss. I've done this before! I know I have. There's no way a novice could do this. Sailing was a big part of my life. I can't remember why. I'll have to think about it later.

We crash through another swell, and I turn my attention back to keeping Icebreaker upright and afloat. Just as Stirling's electric violin fades, I catch a glimpse of something red. The rolling swells keep the object hidden for what seems like forever, and when it appears again, we're almost on top of it.

"It's a kayak!" I yell to Tonka, who spots it at the same time. "And there's something in it!"

Dropping sail in strong winds and waves is dangerous, but I can't risk crashing into the other boat. Icebreaker founders in the water and I struggle to keep the stern pointed toward the wind. As the next swell passes under us, I praise myself for having lowered sail. If we hadn't, we would have dropped right on top of the kayak...which would have been far more of a disaster than I could have imagined.

"Tonka!" I yell. "There's somebody in that thing! We have to see if they're alive!"

Now the question is, will our luck hold out?

Icebreaker's bow shaves the side of the smaller vessel, and as our portsides slam together, I see the kayaker's face framed by the fur-lined hood of an arctic parka. It could be a young boy or a teen girl. There's not enough detail to be certain. Yet, somehow...call it female intuition...I know it's a girl.

I lean out far as I dare, grasping the cargo webbing on the kayak's bow. A million thoughts race through my mind as I strctch to grab hold of the passenger. Questions that won't be answered if I lose my grip.

By some minor miracle, I reach the girl's shoulder with my hand and latch on. I'm pretty strong for my size, thanks to a winter of woodcutting and hard work. But this is going to be tough. And dangerous. The tempest rages around us. I'll only have one chance to pull this off. I twist my body to grab the other shoulder, then plant my feet against the bulkhead. Like a power lifter, I use my legs to lift with all my strength.

Another swell passes under us, first lifting Icebreaker and then the little red boat. As my cruiser comes down the back side of the swell, it is...for an instant...lower than the kayak. The girl I'm holding on to comes out of the skirted passenger compartment like a cork and we land in a heap on the deck. By the time I sit up and look over the gunwale, the little vessel has filled with water. I only get a glimpse as it slides beneath the murky river water. Any personal possessions or valuables inside are lost forever.

A klaxon in my head blasts a warning! Icebreaker will be swamped if I don't raise sail..and I have no desire to become a submarine. Cranking on the halyard winch like a madwoman, the sail rises up the mast...a difficult and dangerous task with the gale whipping across my starboard beam. The sail catches the wind, and the response is immediate. We are moving again!

The girl at my feet moans, but there's nothing I can do now. I can't take Tonka to the cabin because I can't leave the tiller. The thrill and joy of sailing Icebreaker through the storm has vanished. Now it's a race to make it home to save this girl's life.

"I can't believe it!" I yell to Tonka, myself, and the wide, empty world. "Another person! Another human being. Alive! I hope it's not too late. It can't be too late."

At least the wind direction is in our favor. Icebreaker takes a pounding and the spray washes over us with each wave, but we're making good time. We reach our little creek and I dock the boat without turning it around. Priority one is to take care of the castaway.

The nor'easter has pushed water into the creek, so Icebreaker is riding higher than usual. This means I can lower the castaway onto the dock instead of lifting. Thank goodness for small favors.

I untether Tonka and place him on the dock. Now for the hard part. I jump out of the boat and remove the garden wagon's side panels, turning it into a mini-flatbed. I position the wagon next to the boat and climb back on board and, using leverage, maneuver the castaway onto the gunwale.

With one hand on the slumping girl, I step onto the dock and tip her upper torso, back first, onto the wagon. From there, it's a simple matter of lowering her legs and centering her body so she won't fall off the wagon. Simple, but exhausting.

The girl's thick clothing conceals how big she is, but she appears to be the same size as me. I'm just glad it's not someone who weighs a ton. If we were forced to stay on the sailboat, caring for the survivor would be a nightmare.

I take a deep breath and begin pulling the wagon to the house, Tonka leading the way. We pass Challenger, stop at the center stairwell, and open the door. I look at the girl and then the stairs. This is going to be tough. Really tough. There's no way I can lift this kind of weight straight from the wagon. There has to be a way to do this.

"The Krav Maga carry!" I say to Tonka, the memory of the technique breaks through the barrier preventing me from remembering so many things. "I can do this!"

Wait! I know Krav Maga..the martial art used by the Israel Defense Forces?

Once triggered, the unsummoned memory of the carry technique led to remembering the name of the self-defense style. Sort of a dominos effect. My mixed-up mind is like a box of Cracker Jack...you never know what kind of surprise you'll find inside.

The technique uses leverage similar to the way I maneuvered the survivor off the sailboat. I pivot her legs and upper torso in succession so she is in a sitting position. Next, I sit on her lap, then drape her arms over my shoulders and around my neck. I plant my feet on the concrete, lean forward so the weight is on my back, then stand. I can lift the girl because I'm using my legs, not my arms or back.

It's not easy carrying a person up steps, but it's doable. When we reach the top of the stairs, I keep going until we reach the master bedroom. As gently as I can, I let the girl slide off my back onto the bed. Once I've caught my breath, I make sure the girl is still breathing, then begin removing her wet clothes.

At last, I pull back the parka's hood and take my first look at...her! She's definitely a girl. She's alive...and I'm going to do everything I can to keep her that way.

CHAPTER TWENTY

Then There Were Two

Tonka doesn't poke me until well past sunrise. He has an urgent look that means he needs to go out. Swinging my legs onto the floor turns my calves, quads and hamstrings into flaming knots of fire. My arms are twenty-pound weights. It takes a moment to gather myself and to collect my thoughts.

"What the heck is wrong with me?" I ask Tonka. "It feels like I fell down a flight of stairs."

The kayaker! Memories of climbing the stairs with the girl on my back and all the exertions it took to rescue her flash through my mind. After dropping her on the bed, there was still heavy lifting to do. It's not easy to remove soaking wet winter clothes from someone who's unconscious. And underneath those, she was wearing a wetsuit. Geez Louise, a wetsuit sticks to skin like it's made with a million little suction cups. That was a job!

After removing her clothes, I had to towel her off and maneuver her under the covers. Not as hard as picking her up, but rolling a body from side to side isn't so easy peasy. While tucking her legs under the sheets, I noticed a tattoo on the outside of her right ankle. A sun symbol in the style used by Native Americans. A Zia, my sporadic memory tells me. Perhaps a tribute to her ancestry?

The rest of the evening was divided between taking care of myself...showering, cooking, eating, feeding Tonka...and keeping an eye on her. She remained unconscious, but at least there were no signs of injury or sickness. She appears to be in good health, with one exception.

The girl has a growth of fine hair over most of her body and her skin was dry and yellowish...all signs of an eating disorder. The hair on her head was too wet to tell if it was brittle...another one of the symptoms...but it looked thin for a young woman. And her body mass is off. She's too thin, not exactly anorexic, but eating two or five cheeseburgers wouldn't be a bad thing.

My exertions weren't just physical, I paid a mental price as well. A million theories, concerns and fears had burned through my brain like a wildfire and my emotions were a series of ups and downs that would make a roller coaster envious. Who is she? Where is she from? What's her name? Where was she going? Where has she been living? How did she survive? Does she know other survivors?

Exhausted, I hit the wall, crashed on the sofa at about eight o'clock, and didn't wake until now. I'd slept for almost twelve hours.

A sudden wave of comprehension slaps me to attention. Twelve hours! Is she still OK?

All the aches and soreness dragging me down a moment ago are dashed away by adrenalin. I cross the room to the bedroom in two bounding steps and...come to an abrupt stop! The girl is sitting up in bed, pointing my pistol at my head.

"Who are you?" she asks, stone-faced and unwavering. "Where am I?"

My heart is about to beat its way out of my chest, and my mouth refuses to form words. It had never occurred to me to remove my weapons. Making matters worse, I can see by the way she's holding the pistol, she doesn't know what she's doing.

Tonka brushes against my leg and growls at the girl. Her eyes cut away from mine to look down at the terrier. This is bad. Very bad.

"Ivy Moon!" The words come out as a shriek, startling the girl, snapping her attention back to me. "My name is...is Ivy Moon, and I saved your life. Please, take your finger off the trigger. It's pretty sensitive and I really don't want to die today."

The girl's eyes narrow. Her mind working, trying to decide if it's some kind of trick.

"It's one of the basic rules of gun safety," I say, trying to keep her from thinking too much. "Never put your finger on the trigger unless you're going to shoot. Rest it on the frame above the trigger guard. If you're going to use a weapon, you need to learn how to handle it the right way. Safely."

It takes a couple of moments, but she moves her finger off the trigger.

"What's your name?" I ask, wanting to keep her engaged on my terms, not hers.

"I...I don't know," she says. The hardness in her face relaxes a little, shifting to uncertainty and anguish.

"For real?" I say, seeing a way to win her over. "I can't remember my name either. Not my real name. Ivy Moon is the name I gave myself after I...gained consciousness after the storm."

"You have amnesia, too?" she says. Her body relaxes a little more, and she lowers the pistol so it's no longer pointing at me.

"Yes, amnesia. I can't remember anything from before the storm. Well, not personal things about myself. I only remember things I learned in school or learned in life. Nothing about who I am or my family or where I'm from. You know? The stuff that really matters."

"Me too," the kayaker says, letting her pistol hand rest on the bed beside her. "I can only remember things that have happened since the storm. I woke up in the back of an ambulance outside the clinic at

Cherry Point. It was weird. The engine was running, but everyone was gone. I think they were going to transport me to a hospital off-base or something. I had blood on my clothes and bandages wrapped around my head."

"Have you found any other people?" I ask, relaxing a little. Her body language says she's beginning to trust me, but part of my attention remains laser-focused on her hand with the pistol.

"No... Well, maybe. I'm not sure. Yesterday or the day before, I...wait. How long have I been here?"

"I pulled you out of the kayak yesterday," I say.

"OK, so, two days ago, I saw a sailboat go by the place I live...or, at least I saw the sail. By the time I got to the river, it was too far away to see if anyone was on it. I've seen several boats drift by, but this was the first one I've seen with the sails up. I have to believe someone was in it."

"It had to be me," I say. "I was on my way to Beaufort. I spotted you yesterday on my way back here."

She mulled this over for a moment, playing out the timing and realizing how incredible it was we had crossed paths at all.

"That's crazy," she says, still looking down in thought. "I was mad at myself for not being better prepared. It took me most of the day to round up the kayak, carry it to the river, and load it with food and water. And then I had to find the right gear to wear. I swore that when morning came, I was going to search for the sailboat no matter what. When I woke up yesterday, I was so desperate to start my search I hardly noticed the weather."

"You were unconscious when I found you. I almost sailed right over you. I could have killed you...by accident, I mean."

"It happens," she says. "Sometimes I pass out, sometimes I'll go to bed and sleep for like twelve hours or more. It may be because of the head injury. Being hungry or exhausted seems to trigger it. I was so ramped up after seeing your boat I forgot to eat."

"You haven't eaten in two days?"

"At least," she says. "To be honest, I...I've been pretty depressed the past two or three months, you know? Not having anybody to talk to. Not knowing if there was anyone else alive."

CHAPTER TWENTY-ONE

Roxie

"Breakfast is served," I say, entering the bedroom with a tray of food. "Sorry it took so long, but Tonka was doing a pee dance and had to go out."

The girl's eyes grow wide at the smorgasbord of food loaded on the really cool bed tray the homeowners left behind. The handgun is laying on the end table beside her.

"We've got cheese-eggs, bacon, fried ham, grits, toast with jam, raisin bran, cold milk, peaches, and a stack of pancakes with syrup and butter."

"How?" she asks, stunned by the display. "Where? I mean, I know there's plenty of food out there, but milk, cheese, eggs and butter?"

"Well," I say, doing my best fake-modesty eye-lash flutter, "I cheated. The eggs and milk are powdered. The cheese comes out of a jar. The ham and the peaches come from a can. The bacon is precooked stuff with a long shelf life. The butter is flavored flakes from a shaker. And the toast is really flatbread. The preserves and grits are real, though."

"Still, this is amazing!"

She picks up the glass of milk and takes a sip.

"It really is cold! How?"

"Well, it's easy, if you have power."

"You have electricity?"

"Yeah. Solar panels, but they don't power the entire house. The refrigerator stays on all the time. I have to switch circuits around to use other things. I'll show you how the control panel works when you feel better."

She sets the glass on the tray and stares at the food. Her mind is working overtime, struggling with something.

"Why are you being so nice to me?" she asks, looking up at me. "A little while ago, I pulled a gun on you. I could have killed you. Yet, here you are still taking care of me, feeding me. I don't deserve it."

Instead of answering her question, I giggle. The look on her face is a mix of confusion and resentment.

She no doubt believes she's come face to face with a deranged psycho killer.

"I'm sorry," I say, still giggling, "but you have one of the best milk mustaches ever."

She picks up a knife and looks at her reflection in the blade. Her face turns red with embarrassment, but then grins.

"You've got to be kidding," I say, as she wipes her mouth with a napkin. "Why am I helping you? Until yesterday, I thought I was the last person on earth. Surviving hasn't been hard, but the loneliness was unbearable. If you are the only other person left alive, we need to be friends. We have to be friends."

She nods in agreement and begins sampling the food on her tray. After the first forkful of cheese-eggs goes down, she doesn't stop feeding her face for several minutes. This girl has rediscovered her appetite.

"Yeah, I get it," she says, pausing long enough to gulp down half the milk. "I was already losing it. That's why I hadn't been eating. I mean, when you're the only person left, what's the point of living, right?"

It's a legit question. One if dwelled upon too long could drive a person mad.

"We have a lot to talk about," I say, turning the conversation in a more positive direction. "But first things first."

"Which is what?" she asks, not noticing my re-direct.

"We've got to give you a name. I can't be saying, 'hey you' all the time."

She smiles, but doesn't reply. She's too focused on the ham and grits.

"I'm thinking we should come up with a name associated with your location or a significant event you've experienced. How does Cherry Point work? Or just Cherry? That's where I found you...on the river. Just off the base."

"Cherry!" she shoots back. But with her mouth full, it sounds more like Wary. "No thanks!"

"OK!" I laugh. "I think I understand. It sounded good in my head. Do you have any ideas?"

"Not really. I never thought about it. At first, I figured it would come back to me pretty quick. If not, I'd find other people who could tell me. As time went by, not having a name didn't matter, because there was no one around to tell it to."

"I hear you. I would have felt the same way if not for Tonka. He's like the coolest dog that's ever lived."

Tonka's ears perk up at hearing his name and raises his head. He's been resting in the doorway listening to us talk and watching the food disappear from the breakfast tray.

"Where did you find him?" she asks.

"He was here when I broke in. Look out the window. See that? It's the mast of the boat I was on. Challenger. You'll see the whole boat when you go on the porch. It drifted right up to the back steps when the yard was flooded. When I jumped from the boat to the porch, I fell into the water and almost drowned. But this little guy was here when I got inside. We've been helping each other survive ever since."

"I wonder if I've ever had a pet," the girl says. "Do you think he'll like me?"

"I'm sure he will. He just needs to get to know you. Don't rush it. He'll come around when he's ready."

She nods and finishes the last of the food. As I pick up the tray and turn to leave, the wetsuit hanging on the closet door catches my attention.

"Wait a minute," I say. "The name tag on the wetsuit says Roxie. But that's not your gear, right?"

"Yeah, that's right. I found it with a bunch of other wetsuits in a recreation building on base. Most of them had name tags, that one just happened to fit me."

"Well, how does the name Roxie sound? Roxie River...you know...because I found you on the river."

"Roxie River," she says slowly. "Hmmm..."

"Well, I like it," I say. "It sounds sort of like Rocky River, which is kinda cool. And it's relevant to your birth. That's what I call my crawling out of the sailboat and seeing the world for the first time. The first day I have memory of, so to say. It may not be when I was born, but it's when this part of my life began."

"Roxie River," she says again, trying the name on for size. "Rox-ie...Riv-er."

As I walk to the kitchen with the tray, my heart is soaring. An hour ago, the girl...Roxie...sounded like a candidate for a suicide intervention. Now, she has a name and hope in her voice.

"Ivy!" she calls to me as I clean the dishes.

"Yeah?" I say, fearing my celebration had been premature.

"Thank you!"

Now my spirits are over the moon! It's a new day, for sure. There are so many questions to ask and survival notes we need to compare. The answers will come as Roxie recovers. In the meantime, I'm happier and more energized than I've been since the storm.

By the time the dishes are done, Roxie is sleeping again, which is a good thing. Rest and food are exactly what she needs. Only, from now on, she shouldn't eat so much at one sitting. That could present its own problems.

To take advantage of the downtime, Tonka and I head out to the boat to perform some maintenance. The Westie watches from the dock while I clean Icebreaker, square away the cabin and deck, and then reposition her so the bow is pointing outbound. Be prepared, right! I really am a good girl scout.

It's well past noon when we return to the house for lunch. As we step inside, we're greeted by the whine of a small motor coming from the kitchen. Intrigued, I turn the corner to see Roxie standing in front of a makeup mirror, blow-drying her hair. The white bathrobe she's wearing provides vivid contrast to her long black strands. Color has returned to her skin, which is darker than I had thought, and she already looks healthier. She turns off the dryer and sees us as she reaches for a hairbrush.

"You must be feeling better," I say.

"Yes, thanks to you! I took a shower and brought this stuff in here to dry my hair because there's no power in the bathroom. I hope you don't mind."

"Of course not," I say as I open a can of mushroom soup and pour the contents into a pot. "I do it sometimes, too. I'll show you how to switch power from one zone to another after lunch. Is there anything else you need?"

"No, thanks," she says, running the brush through her hair. "Well, actually, I'm going to need some clothes to wear. Everything I had was on the kayak. Can you help a girlfriend out?"

"No problem," I say, smiling at the idea I have an honest-to-gosh BFF. "You're a little taller than me, but I'm sure I have some things you can wear. We can go shopping for your size later."

"Shopping?" she laughs. "Like, you have open stores here?"

"Well, technically, everything downtown is open," I say with a smile. "But 'shopping' is my euphemism for salvaging. I have a list of places around here with clothes you might like."

"Euphemism," she says, raising her eyebrows. "That's a ten-dollar word. Are you a brainiac or something?"

"No!" I say, a bit too defensively. My eyes remain focused on cutting up the leftover canned meat from breakfast and adding it to the soup. "Well, to be honest, I guess I am a little nerdy. But I don't think I'm a genius or anything."

"Nothing wrong with being a brainiac or a genius. As long as we're being up front, I think I'm a little nerdy, too. And look at it logically. If we weren't on the higher end of the WAIS scale, we probably wouldn't have survived this long, right?"

"The Wechsler Adult Intelligence Scale?" I say. "Now who's the brainiac?"

We both laugh and look at each other for a moment in the "nice getting to know you" sort of way. This girl has potential.

"Your skin," I say, taking advantage of the moment. "It's very brown. Any idea what your heritage is?

"Not a clue. I wonder the same thing almost every time I look in the mirror, but...who knows? What do you think?"

"Oh, I'm terrible at this sort of thing," I say, though I have no memories of ever having guessed people's heritage or ethnicity. "You have prominent cheekbones, almond-shaped eyes, and dark hair. You could be Native American, which would be cool because River sounds like a name an American Indian might have. Or maybe you're an Asian-American mix like Kelsey Chow."

"For real?" she says, putting the brush down to look in the mirror. "She's like, beautiful. Thanks!"

"Well, you are pretty. I think you'll look even better when you gain some weight...no offense."

"None taken," she says with a chuckle. "But even after I do put on a few pounds, I won't look as good as you. And as long as we are comparing each other to actors, you have a Katheryn Winnick, Lagertha Viking-girl vibe that totally works for you."

"Oh?" I say, embarrassed. "If you say so."

After all these months, I still haven't taken a good look at myself in a mirror. It's a weird phobia, I know. But it's real, and it's mine. It's not hard to avoid taking in my entire reflection when I look in a mirror. I just focus on the part I need to see and never step back to take in my whole face at once. Yeah, weird.

She doesn't notice my pause because I'm ladling up the hot soup.

"And you must be ripped," she continues, "or whatever word people use to describe really toned girls. How the heck did little you carry me up those stairs?"

"It wasn't easy, trust me. It was more about leverage than brute strength. But, yeah, I'm in pretty good shape. Comes with chopping firewood and doing all the heavy lifting around here. You'll find out soon enough."

"Will I?" she asks. Her shoulders slump and she averts her eyes. "You want me to hang around? I didn't make my best first impression earlier...pointing a gun at you. I'm really sorry about that, especially now I know how kind and giving you are. More than sorry, I'm ashamed."

"Forget it," I say, "but no more gun handling until I teach you a few things. Got it?"

"Yeah. I promise. I'm pretty sure I never even held a gun in my life before the storm. When I picked up the pistol and pointed it at you, I was scared to death."

"I understand. We do what we have to do to survive. I carry weapons because I've learned it's dangerous not to. I'm not sure how things are at Cherry Point, but we have all kinds of bears, wolves and coyotes running around here. You don't want to be caught unprepared."

"Wow!" she says, interrupting the flow of conversation. "You can cook! This soup is crazy good."

"It's the processed ham," I say. "Way too much salt, but the soup is low-sodium, so it balances out. And the other spices in the ham enhance the mushroom flavor. But...I think you were going to say something about Cherry Point?"

"I'm afraid there's not much to tell. I haven't been as adventurous as you. I mostly stay on base, either at the event center or a giant house downriver a little way. It was some general's house, I think."

"An event center?"

"Yeah, it has tons of food all in one place and gas stoves to cook on. I feel safer there for some reason. Plus, it gives me an excellent view of the river. You know, to keep a lookout for any boats passing by."

"Well, that'll change if you stick with me. I have a curious nature. I'm compelled to see what's around the next bend. Most of all, I need to know if there are other survivors out there. I found you, right? So we know it's possible."

"Are you sure it's the best thing to do? I mean, I almost killed you, and I'm not even a bad person. What if we come across people who aren't like us?"

"I've thought about it a lot," I say, finishing my soup. "I know it's not without risk. But I believe the risk is worth it, especially if we find people who can explain what happened and if there are other survivors. That said, if we do make contact, we need to use extreme caution. Find out who they are and what they're about before trusting them."

"We need to make a plan!" Roxie says, excitement growing in her voice. "Not just one plan, several plans. Create scenarios and figure out the best ways to react."

"Now you're talking," I say. "We can even walk through them, role play, make sure each of us can do the other person's job. But first, we need to round up some more weapons and familiarize you with them. Practice...then train."

Roxie goes silent, her eyes darting about as she tries to nail down a single thought to focus on. She's stoked.

"There's one scenario we can make a rule for right now," I say. "In the future, if we bring somebody into our space...we don't leave weapons around where they can pick them up and use them against us. Deal?"

Her focus locks back on me, hurt in her eyes. But when she sees my smile, the pain vanishes and we both laugh.

CHAPTER TWENTY-TWO

Emma Stone Eyes

I love Roxie, but sometimes she's an enigma. Most days she's rock solid, industrious, irresistible, and fun. This version of her is the real Roxie. I could have gone to "BFFs are Us" and couldn't have ordered a better post-apocalypse survival friend.

Then there are the dark, moody days when she's ambling about with no sense of purpose or direction. I've come to use these shifts in temperament as a barometer of sorts. On every occasion when these moods arise, she suffers a blackout within the day. To say these episodes are disconcerting is an understatement. If she blacks out at the wrong time...like when driving the golf cart...the result could be disastrous. So, on those days when she's not herself, I steer her away from risky tasks.

The truth is, we're both fractured people doing the best we can. The accident of our existence is a circumstance we can't ignore. It's the bond we share above all else. Though we never talk about it, the knowledge we still exist while...as far as we know...no one else does, is always with us. It's equal parts blessing and burden, with a massive portion of guilt mixed in. Why us? Why are we still here and everybody else is gone?

Talking about it would do no good. There are no answers to these questions. At least, none available to us. Trying to find the answers would be like the horrible way they once baited greyhounds for the races...forever chasing a rabbit they could see, but never catch. Madness.

Instead, we put our effort into productive tasks such as exploring, scavenging, gardening, and raising livestock. Having a partner makes almost everything a lot easier and a lot more fun. By working together...Roxie covers my back while I work the chainsaw...we finish clearing the main road of fallen trees. We are now free to move about the country, as the airline commercial used to say.

Only these days, we travel in style. We keep the golf cart handy for quick trips around the neighborhood, but our primary ride for the open road is a late model pickup truck. It has four doors, a cargo bed, roll bars, step bars, light bars, winch, four-wheel drive, and an overhead gun rack. Sweet!

Thanks to a nifty padded center console, there's plenty of room for all three of us up front. Tonka wouldn't have it any other way and neither would I. Although he and Roxie are getting along, he hasn't shined to her like he does with me. I feel bad for her, but I love Tonka's loyalty.

Being able to reach the state highway means we have access to the farms and stores we need to transition our little house into a productive homestead. In a matter of days, we salvage a tiller, seeds, fertilizer, netting, garden tools, a water pump, hoses and sprinklers. Not only do we have everything we need to plant a vegetable garden, we have the means to build an irrigation system. Not too shabby.

We also score dozens of metal garden posts for the netting. In addition to deer, the population growth of crows, raccoons, squirrels and all kinds of other critters have exploded. We'll never eat the things we grow if we can't keep the animals from eating them first.

The best place to plant vegetable gardens is in the front yards of the houses around the cul-de-sac. The ground is higher and less likely to flood. They're also free of roots and other debris that can damage the tiller. We just have to locate and avoid the underground water, cable and power lines.

It's amazing how much two people can accomplish when they labor from sunrise to sundown. But it's not all hard work. We divide our time between planting the gardens, building pens for goats and a coop for chickens, and fishing.

I'm not talking about fishing with a pole. No way. I'm talking about net fishing. And the first time we try...we crush it! We string a gill net across the mouth of our creek and leave it out for the whole day. And we'll never do it again.

It turns out, the fish are multiplying as fast as the wildlife on land. We catch so many fish the net is too heavy to haul in! And even if we could, there's no way to clean them all or eat them before going bad. Lesson learned. We now limit our fishing to an hour or less, and we always have more than enough. Pretty good for two girls with zero experience...as far as we know.

The same thing happens with crabbing. We start by retrieving ten crab pots left in the water by commercial fishermen. Then we bait them with fish heads and leave them in the river's shallow water overnight. When we come back the next morning, there are so many crabs in each cage it's ridiculous. Never again. It's one crab pot at a time from now on. Even with fake butter, fresh crab is one of the best things I've ever eaten! Especially with a little garlic mixed in.

Noon each day is "Lunch and Learn" time. After teaching Roxie the fundamentals of gun safety and proper procedure, we practice aiming, firing, and tactical techniques. Most of this knowledge pops up from my latent memory, but I also check myself by pulling up information from the desktop computer files.

The same goes for almost every new skill we employ. Fishing, building, planting. We don't waste learning new skills by trial and error. If we're not sure how to work a nail gun or a saw or whatever, we look it up. We've come to the point we believe we can do just about anything. And why shouldn't we? We rock! Sorry. I don't mean to be conceited. But, hey! If we don't praise ourselves, who will? Nobody. Because there is nobody else, right?

When we're done building the pens and coop, it's time to go in search of goats and chickens. But where to start? At the computer, of course.

This time, we call up satellite mapping and survey the surrounding countryside. It takes only a few minutes to create a list of places likely to have livestock. When we're finished, we pack a lunch and hop into the truck.

It's one of those rare days when everything seems right with the world. We may live in a post-apocalypse, but we're doing alright. We've got the windows rolled down and taking it slow so we can enjoy the ride. Roxie has on earphones, checking out the awesome play lists on the MP-3 player. She's not even paying attention to the scenery. But when we reach the main highway, she taps me on the wrist and asks if she can drive.

"Sure," I say. "Have at it."

It's not the first time she's taken the wheel. She's a natural. But when she slides into the driver's seat, I can't help but notice the big smile on her face. She's up to something. I'm sure of it.

"Enough of this," she says, switching on the Bluetooth speaker sitting on the dashboard. The player connects, and she hits the play button on the MP-3. "How old are you? A hundred and two? Let's get this party started!"

With that, she slams the shifter into drive at the same time Golden Earring's "Radar Love" comes blasting out of the speaker. I'm sure she's squealing tires, but I can't hear anything over the screaming notes of the lead guitar. I yell at her to slow down. She ignores me, tapping her hands on the steering wheel and lip synching the lyrics instead.

I'm livid! I wanna choke her! For real! She could get us all killed. Then, when the music pauses for the drum solo, she turns and give's me a wink.

"What? You afraid we're gonna get a speeding ticket or something?"

OK, she has a point. And she's so into the music, I can't help but laugh. Plus, we're not really going *that* fast. So, why not do a little Livin' la Vida Loca? Oooo... I make a mental note to play the Ricky Martin song later. Now, I join in with Roxie, who's singing the last stanza of "Radar Love" at the top of her lungs. Our perfect day just got better!

We're going slower by the time we reach our first destination, listening to "When God-Fearin' Women get the Blues." What a powerful voice Martina McBride has! Roxie stops the music as we turn onto a dirt road. We drive past a modern farmhouse until we see a huge poultry barn next to a magnificent oak tree. There are no signs of life, but our hopes are high as we step out of the truck and walk closer.

"Oh my god!" Roxie says as we approach the barn. "Gag a maggot! What is that smell?"

It's only a week past spring, but growing hotter each day. Flies are everywhere and the growing humidity seals the stink around us like plastic wrap. It's so disgusting even Tonka...who's been known to roll in deer scat...crinkles his nose.

"That," I say, "is what's left of the chickens inside. It's a huge barn. There must be hundreds of dead birds. As bad as it smells now, it had to be ten times worse nine months ago."

"Those poor creatures," she says. "It's like a chicken apocalypse...an apoultrycalypse."

"What?" I say, with a chuckle, not sure I heard correctly. "Are you seriously cracking a joke about dead chickens?"

"No! Well...maybe a little. Too irreverent? How does apollocaust sound? Armachicken?"

"You're an idiot," I say, struggling to suppress a laugh.

"A coop de grâce?"

"Shut up! Stop it!"

I force myself to quit chuckling and give her a look of disbelief and indignation...but I can't hold it. She sees through my façade and we laugh so hard it hurts. The jokes are both terrible and hilarious. Dark humor only two girls who've been alone too long and too-long deprived of joy can find hysterical.

We laugh so hard tears come to our eyes and we fall to the grass, arms clutching our stomachs. Tonka runs around us, dodging in and out and barking. He doesn't know what's happening, but he wants in on the fun.

We lie on the grass looking skyward until the waves of laughter subside. The sky is as clear and blue as I've ever seen it. A cool breeze delivers relief from the heat, and for a few glorious minutes, our psyches are transported to a time with no worries, no responsibilities. A world much better than it had a right to be. And for a moment, I glimpse what life was like before the storm. Like looking through a veil, seeing the outlines, but not the details.

The spell is broken as the real world shifts back into focus. Earth is a quiet place without humans polluting it with our noise. It's a world of breezes whispering secrets through pine needles, mockingbirds imitating the impolite blue jays, the drone of a thousand bees harvesting pollen.

The sound is so subtle I almost miss its significance. A thousand bees! As in honeybees! With the speed of a sloth, I sit up and look around.

"Roxie," I say, whispering for no apparent reason. "Look, an apiary!"

Off to the left of the poultry barn, under the oak tree, sits a little village of beehives. There are at least a dozen separate stands with varying numbers of boxes stacked on top. The hives are placed between the tree's afternoon shade zone and a few feet from a koi pond.

"I think the big box on the bottom of each hive is called a brood box," Roxie says as we watch hundreds of bees flying to and from the hives. "Each of the narrower boxes above the brood box is a super. That's where the honeycombs are."

"How do you know this stuff?"

"I don't know," she says. "It just came to me. Maybe my family had something to do with beekeeping."

"We have to take one home," I say. "Think about it. We could have fresh honey anytime we want and it will help with our gardens. And I think I remember reading something about, if you eat local honey, it helps prevent allergies."

"Are you crazy?" she says. "You think we can just go over there and pick one of those things up and the bees will be like, 'Cool! Let's go for a ride?'"

"Well, yeah," I say. "But you're the bee expert. How can we do this?"

"I don't know. Bees like this are pretty tame, but you go moving their hive around and they'll get mean real quick. I wouldn't try it without a beekeeper's suit."

"OK. This is a farm, and that's an apiary. They must keep suits around here somewhere. Probably back at the farmhouse."

So, back down the road we go where we spot a large combination garage-storage building tucked behind the farmhouse. It's the type of structure farmers use to keep tractors, implements and supplies. It only takes a few minutes to locate two beekeeper suits in a storage room. We also find something else that will help.

"Look," Roxie says, holding up a round metal canister. "A bee smoker! Now we're talking!"

"You know how to use that thing?"

"I think so," she says, opening up the top of the smoker. "Yeah, look, burnt pine straw. Beekeepers burn it to make the smoke. Just stuff some pine straw inside, light it and you're in business."

"In business to do what?" I ask.

"Smoke the hive. It freaks out the bees inside. They're like, 'We're under attack! We gotta do something! But first, we have to eat a lot of honey for energy!' It also blocks the queen bee's pheromone signals, so everybody inside stays chill."

"How long does it last?"

"Meh. A few minutes. Long enough to lift a hive and put it in the back of the truck. Once it's in the truck bed, we'll throw a tarp over it so the bees will think it's nighttime. If we drive slow, enough bees should survive to keep the hive viable."

"OK, what do we do first?"

"Drive back up to the apiary, put on the suits, and go from there."

When I back the truck up close to the shortest beehive stack, I leave Tonka inside with the air conditioner on and the engine running. They don't make beekeeper suits for little dogs, so I'm not taking any chances. Next, we drop the tailgate and pull on the two-piece suits and hats. We help each other with the hats, closing any gaps in the netting so the bees can't fly through. Tonka sees us through the cab window and growls. We must look like space aliens or swamp creatures.

Made for much bigger people, the suits don't fit very well. Roxie keeps stepping on her pants legs and I feel like I'm swimming in mine. The elastic waistband is worn out and my pants don't have a drawstring. It makes everything we do twice as hard, but we manage to light the pine straw and begin smoking a small hive.

It works! A few bees are still flying around, but we're not being swarmed.

"Easy peasy, lemon squeezy," I say as we lower the hive onto the tailgate and slide it into the bed.

"Did anyone ever tell you how stupid that sounds?" Roxie asks as we pull the tarp over the hive and tie it down. I can't see if she is smiling because of the netting around our faces. "Seriously, it's something a six-year-old would say."

"Well," I shoot back, "who died and left you queen of what I can and can't say?"

She's right, of course. I know it sounds childish. But hearing someone else say what I already know hurts.

"Jeez," she says, "You don't need to get all hostile. I'm just saying, for somebody who's supposed to be a genius, I would think you could come up with a better reduplicative than that. I mean, easy peasy? What would you think if I was always saying, 'okey dokey, wokey smokey?'"

"First off," I say, "why don't you use the word 'lexeme' like a normal person? And second...wokey smokey? That's not a thing."

"Because, Grammar Girl, the word 'lexeme' usually only applies to a single word. And yes, wokey smokey is a thing."

"Since when?"

"Since about two seconds ago."

"Please, just stop."

"Okey dokey, wokey smoky!" she taunts.

"You're an idiot," I say, shaking my head, trying not to laugh.

"Okey dokey, wokey smokey," she says in a sing-song chant, her hips and shoulders moving to the beat. "Let's all do the okey dokey, wokey smokey, hokey pokey..."

Dressed in the beekeeper suit, she looks the complete fool. She knows it and exaggerates her movements for clownish effect. Roxie continues with the childish rhyming and attempts to execute a one-eighty. But her foot catches on the long pants legs and she pitches forward. Only now, "forward" is toward the apiary's closest beehive.

With a crash, she falls into the stack of boxes and knocks them over. The sections come apart and the air fills with the sound of thousands of angry bees swarming around her head. Confused, panicked and unable to see through the bee cloud, she tries to stand, but loses her balance and knocks over another hive.

From where I'm standing, it's like seeing bad special effects in an old monster movie. She's Godzilla and the hives being knocked over are the city's skyscrapers. The bees are like a zillion tiny Mothras attacking her head. I can't help but start laughing.

"It's not funny!" Roxie screams at me as she stands. From the neck down, she has a normal body, but her head is like a weird balloon character that won't come into focus.

"I'm not laughing!" I yell back at her, though I obviously am. "Just be still and let them settle down. You're in a beekeeper suit, remember?"

"I hate you," she yells back, though I can see she is taking my advice. "I'm gonna pay you back for laughing at me. This isn't funny...at all!"

"Aw, come on," I yell over the noise of the bees. "It's all in fun. Remember, it's the okey dokey, wokey smokey, hokey pokey...and you're *really* good at it."

Even through all the bees, I see a calm come over her. The kind of calm people have when they've determined an objective and won't be stopped until they've achieved it. Slowly, so as not to trip again, she comes toward me, oblivious to the bees.

"Roxie, what are you doing?

Instead of answering, she comes closer. I'm not laughing anymore.

"Roxie, don't do anything stupid. Somebody could get hurt."

She continues toward me. I turn to run.

"ROX–" I scream. The second half of her name is cut off when my britches fall around my ankles and I hit the ground face-first, knocking the breath from my lungs.

Having the breath knocked out of you hurts. You can't inhale and you feel you're going to die. The only thing that can make it worse is someone laughing at you hysterically.

"Oxrie..." I gasp, mangling my words. "Elp me..."

Roxie continues laughing, but now I feel a new pain. A lot of new pains. Bees are attacking my bare legs and stinging me. Some have crawled under my coat and sting me there too. I'm freakin' out. They're going to climb up around my chest and face!

"Roxie!" I scream.

But Roxie just laughs harder. Now it's my turn to be mad.

I roll over a couple of times to squash the bees on me, then spring to my feet and pull up my britches as best I can. Roxie is laughing so hard she doesn't see what I'm doing. One giant step brings me next to where she is standing. Before she can react, I bend over and pull her britches down. The bees dive bomb her legs not covered by her shorts and she slaps at them like she's on fire.

"That did it!" she yells.

Without missing a beat in her slapping antics, she takes a swing at my head and knocks off my hat and face netting. A nanosecond after comprehending what she's done, I retaliate, yanking off her headgear. I swear, it's an instinctive act, inflicted without thinking. But, hey! All's fair in love and war, right? And this is war!

If true, then this is a war between two idiots who realize they've been extraordinarily stupid. In unison, we pull up our britches and start running toward the koi pond...the bee swarm attacking us the whole way. We hit the water and dive beneath the surface to escape the bees. The next few minutes is a series of coming up for air, ducking under the water, and swimming as far as we can to lose them before resurfacing. It seems to take forever, but when the bees are satisfied we're no longer a threat, they return to their wrecked hives. Exhausted, Roxie and I crawl onto the grassy bank and collapse, our chests heaving as we catch our breath.

"Thab was bretty stubid," I say, my words distorted by swollen lips.

"Yeb, ib was," she says. "Leb's nod eber do tat again."

"Dealb!" I say.

Able to breathe again, we sit up and look at each other. Roxie points at me and starts laughing...then stops because of the pain.

"Youb got Emba Stone eyes," she says. I know she's right, because I can barely see through the slits they've become.

"Oh yeb. Whalb, youb loog like Angablina Joblee on sterbroids."

We sound ridiculous, and we laugh at ourselves despite the pain...but only for a moment. Everything hurts and we need to go to the truck to administer first aid. Tonka barks at us as we approach the cab, then jumps to the backseat as we climb in. It's going to be a long, slow, painful trip home.

TWENTY-THREE

Lost Girls

We've only traveled about a mile when Roxie groans and slumps against the passenger door. Any other time, I wouldn't be worried. I've gotten used to her blackouts. But this one wasn't preceded by a mood swing. I have to believe it was brought on by the bee stings. If she's going into anaphylactic shock, we've got serious problems.

On the positive side, we're close to the grocery store we use to restock food supplies. At the opposite end of the little strip mall it's in, there's also a drugstore. If luck is with me today, there should be some epinephrine autoinjectors inside. And if not, the grocery store has soap, bottled water and vinegar we can use to treat the stings. We don't have to go all the way home to start first aid.

Parking the truck as close to the drugstore's front door as possible, I dash inside and go behind the counter. The layout looks straightforward. The drugs are shelved in alphabetical order, or so it seems. I go to the E section and...no joy. There's Elbasvir, Eletriptan, Enasidenib and other drugs starting with an E, but no epinephrine. A quick glance around reveals an unexpected wrinkle to the setup. There's another whole shelf system that repeats the alphabet. Some of the drugs are different. Some are the same. Very confusing. As my gaze continues around the room, I see a third set of shelves with yet another A to Z filing of drugs. What's going on here?

"Think, Ivy," I say aloud to help me focus. "There has to be a method behind this madness. What is it?"

My eyes shift from one set of shelves to the next, and back again. The first drug in the first row of bins is Abacavir. The first A drug in the next setup is also Abacavir. Cheese-and-rice! What the heck is going on here? The first A drug in the third set of shelves is Abaloparatide. Why do the first two shelves have the same drug but not the third?

I don't have a clue what any of these drugs are or what they're for, but there must be a reason Abacavir is in the first two sequences, but not the third. Picking up a bottle from the first bin and a bottle from the second, I shake them. The first one rattles. It contains pills or tablets. The second one makes sloshing noises. It's a liquid.

"So, what's in the Abaloparatide bin?" I ask aloud while stepping over to the third sequence. Tipping the bin toward me reveals a stack of boxes. The labeling says, Abaloparatide: injection.

"Booya!" Solids, liquids, and injectors! That's the key to the system. Mystery solved!

It takes about two seconds to locate the epinephrine injectors in the third row of bins and dump the entire supply into a plastic grocery bag. Doing my imitation of The Flash, I race toward the front door, grabbing an enormous bottle of calamine lotion on the way and shove it into the bag. I blast out the front door like it's not even there and...come to a dead stop.

Why? WHY can't I ever think before I do things? Standing between me and the truck are three girls...all with handguns...all of them pointed right at me. I'm an idiot!

"Oh my god!" says the girl in the middle. "What happened to your face? You have some kind of disease?"

All three girls take a step back at the same time, creating more space between us. My free hand goes to my cheek without thinking. My skin is on fire and there are swollen lumps all over my face. I must look like a giant infected golf ball.

In the moment they take to recover, I assess the three ambushers. The girl in the middle is a tall, thin, athletic-looking older teen with dark skin and straight black hair. She's probably the leader because she's the one asking the questions. The girl to her left is my height and size, with wavey copper hair and straw-colored skin. Her facial features are distinctly Asian. She is the most exotic-looking person I've ever seen. The girl on the leader's right is short for her age or barely a teen. It's hard to tell. She has long blonde hair, a great tan, and vivid blue eyes that never waiver. A blonde, a brunette and a redhead...isn't that convenient? It's like they came right out of central casting.

Shorty and the redhead have holsters strapped on their hips and Stretch has a holster under her arm, police detective style. But the holsters are empty because the guns are in their hands, pointed at me. My weapon is holstered...and sitting on the floor of the back seat...where I left it when I put on the beekeeper suit.

"There's somebody in the truck," Red says, looking through the passenger-side window. "She looks as sick as this one. Heck, she might be dead."

Now I'm worried the red-haired girl might do something bad to Roxie or my dog or both. The engine is still running with the AC on and the windows rolled up. Roxie is slumped against the door...which is locked. But the driver's-side door isn't. Seeing a strange face in the window, Tonka's hackles stand on end and he growls.

"Seriously, what's wrong with you two?" Stretch asks again. She's got to be at least six feet tall. "You got something we can catch?"

"Maybe," I say, not sure which way this will go. A "yes" answer might convince them to leave us alone...or they might decide that Roxie and I are dying, so why not put us out of our misery? We practiced responses for a lot of "first contact" scenarios, but none of them included a situation where we're both unarmed and one of us is unconscious. I'm forced to wing it.

"What's in the bag?" the petite blonde asks. She draws out the last word like it has two syllables, a true Southern girl. "Cosmetics? Sweety, it's going to take a five-gallon can of foundation to fix that face."

The plastic bag with the injectors and bottle of lotion hangs heavy against my leg. I completely forgot I was holding it.

"Drugs," I say, not offering any details. Volunteering too much information doesn't seem like a smart play.

"Hey, what's under the tarp?" Red asks, nodding toward the back of the truck.

"Uh, I wouldn't move that if I were you," I say, realizing too late that my comment could be taken as a threat instead of a warning.

"Oh, really?" she says. "Got something special under there? Something that we could use, maybe?"

Red grasps the tarp and pulls it back. At the same time, Shorty steps toward me and reaches for the bag in my hand.

"Seriously," I say, "you're not gonna like it."

I let Shorty take the bag. Resisting would do no good and it leaves me with two free hands. Red is looking at the exposed beehive but doesn't understand what she sees. She pokes it with the barrel of her handgun.

The swarm of bees that explode from the hive is so swift and loud it even scares me. Red and Stretch scream and take off running in opposite directions. Distracted by all the commotion, Shorty is looking toward the truck. So I wrench the gun from her hand...*a Krav Maga move?*...and grab her wrist with a come-along hold. She has no choice but to follow as I back into the drug store. Shoving the pistol into the front of my shorts, I open the door and go inside...only now I don't have to force Shorty to follow. The bees are buzzing all around her and she's desperate to get away. She trips and tumbles to the floor as the door closes behind her.

About a dozen bees make it inside and we swat at them like crazy. Spotting a half-sized cardboard poster of Lisa Rinna modeling adult diapers, I pick it up and start swinging at every bee that comes my way. This goes on for a couple of minutes until I swat down the last of the little kamikazes and pause to take a breath.

"Good job!" I say to Lisa, returning the poster to where I found it. "I couldn't have done it without you. Now, where did Shorty go?"

I look about the room but...nothing. She couldn't have gone outside without me seeing her. I hold my breath and listen.

From the other side of the shelves, I hear labored breathing and a groan. Dashing around the end cap to the next aisle, I see Shorty sprawled on the floor, her face blue and her lips puffed up like balloons. Dropping to my knees, I pick up her arm to take her pulse. Wrapped around her wrist is a red band made of paracord with a metal medical alert tag woven into it. Laid into the center of the tag is a white and red Star of Life emblem. Inside the star is the Rod of Asclepius. The words BEE STING are above the star and the word ALLERGY underneath.

This girl is in shock, which tells me two things. It means that Roxie's blackout was triggered by the stings and isn't having an allergic reaction. She doesn't have the symptoms. Second, if Shorty doesn't get an epinephrine shot stat, she's going to die.

Grabbing the plastic bag she still grasps in her hand, I fish out one of the autoinjector boxes, tear it open, and remove the pen's safety cap. Placing the injector over the meaty part of her upper thigh, I cock my arm back.

"Stop!" the voice belonging to Stretch booms from behind me. "You touch her, you die!"

I don't have to turn around to know that she's pointing her gun at my back.

"Look," I say, lifting Shorty's arm with my free hand. "This is a medical alert tag. I'm sure you must have noticed it before now. It says she's allergic to bee stings. She's gone into anaphylactic shock, which means, if I don't inject her with this epinephrine in the next few seconds...she will die...and it will be your fault."

I still haven't turned around, but I can almost hear the wheels in her head turning.

"Anna electric what?" she asks at last.

"Oh, for pity's sake," I say, exasperated. "I'm going to jab her with this autoinjector on her thigh. She might feel a little pain and she might make some sounds. Shoot me afterward if you want, but I'm doing this. You can thank me later...if I'm still alive."

I slam the nose of the injector into Shorty's thigh before Stretch has time to think. The blonde girl grunts and lets out a moan. And then, like magic, the tension in her body relaxes. The color starts returning to her face and lips. It worked!

"I think I saw some bottles of liquid electrolytes a couple of aisles over," I say, placing my hand on Shorty's forehead. "Go grab some, will ya?"

I don't turn to look, but I'm sure Stretch gives Red a nod, a silent order to fetch the liquid. From the corner of my eye, I see Red take off to search for the electrolytes. Yep, Stretch is definitely the leader.

Red returns with a bottle and hands it to me. I twist the cap off and let Shorty take a few sips. She sits up and looks around.

"What in blue blazes happened?" she asks.

"You almost died," I say, grasping her wrist to take her pulse. "It's a good thing you're wearing a medical alert tag. And it's a good thing I already had the autoinjectors. A few minutes longer and I'm not sure you would have made it."

"Who are you?" Stretch asks.

I don't have a watch, so I don't know what Shorty's heart rate is. But her pulse is strong. And the beat rate is in the right zone...not too slow, not too fast. When I feel satisfied she's going to be alright, I turn to look at Stretch.

"I don't tend to answer people who are pointing a gun at me," I say, glancing toward the hand cannon she's holding. The dang thing must be a Desert Eagle or something.

"Hell's bells, Charlotte, did she really save my life?" Blondie asks.

"Yeah, it seems she did," Stretch says.

"Then I say she's OK," Shorty says. "You need to holster your weapon. You know it's the right thing."

"I agree," Red says. "She kinda even risked her life to do it. She didn't know for sure you weren't going to shoot her. Heck, I wasn't sure."

Stretch studies me for a minute, reviewing the sequence of events in her mind's eye.

"What about the bees?" she says, more accusation than question.

"She did warn us," Red says. "I'm the one who poked the hive."

Stretch takes a deep breath, then slides the huge handgun into the holster under her left arm.

"Excellent decision," a voice at the front of the store declares.

We all turn to see Roxie with her back against the front door frame, her pistol pointing at Stretch. She looks weak and pale, but she's OK. And if my face looks anything like hers, it's no wonder that the three newbies believe we're sick.

The three girls stare at Roxie, realizing they would already be dead if she had wanted to kill them. They still could be. But Roxie lowers her weapon to her side, her arm giving out like she had been holding a fifty-pound dumbbell.

Everybody exhales. It's understood that things could have ended in disaster. People could have died...on both sides. In the end, everyone chose wisely. And the fact we did opens the door to establishing trust. Not that I'm ready to form a sisterhood, but the foundation for acceptance has been laid.

"My name is Ivy Moon," I say. "I don't know where I'm from, originally, but now we live about ten minutes from here. This is my friend Roxie River. She's from Cherry Point, as far as we know. I'll go ahead and tell you that these are made-up names. We both came to after the hurricane last year with amnesia. We don't remember our real names or anything about ourselves before the storm. And you guys?"

The three girls give each other a "you gotta be kidding me" look. Then Stretch takes the lead.

"My name is Charlotte, and like you, we made up our names. I found myself in the 'Queen City' after the storm, with no memories. I have no idea if that's where I was born. I didn't think about adopting a name for myself until I met Goldie."

"Charlotte and I came together...literally...about six months ago when she was passing through Goldsboro," the Asian-looking girl with red hair says, taking over the introduction. "She almost killed me blowing through an intersection downtown at about a hundred miles an hour."

"I was driving a Lamborghini," Charlotte says, as if that explained everything.

"I actually ran into her, but it was only because she was going so fast. One second there was no one on the road and the next second she's a blur zipping by right in front of my face. If I had moved into the intersection one second sooner, she would have hit me broadside and we'd both be dead."

"You've got to get over that," Charlotte says. "I said I was sorry."

Goldie rolls her eyes and continues.

"Anyway, I clipped the back end of her car and she did about four three-sixties before coming to a stop. I lost the front bumper on my car. It came off like a slice of cheese on a cutting board. When I got to Charlotte's car, she was unconscious and I pulled her out."

"My hero," the tall girl says with exaggerated adoration.

"As you can tell, we've been best of friends ever since."

The way they interact is telling. Their banter is good-natured ribbing that only friends can engage in without being offended.

"Neither one of us had names at that point," Goldie continues. "Didn't see a need for one until we got together. Coming up with her name was easy. She had traveled from Charlotte, so...sort of a no-brainer, right?"

"Well, the city was named after Queen Charlotte, King George the Third's wife," the tall girl says. "I can see me being a queen."

"She also sees herself as being our leader," Goldie says, "and we let her think that because it's just easier that way."

"Whatever," Charlotte says.

"From there, it didn't require a lot of imagination to go from her name to mine. Goldsboro wasn't going to work, but I liked the idea of 'Goldie' and I liked the sound of it."

"But–" I start to say.

"I know," she says, cutting me off. "I have copper hair and apparently a lot of Asian DNA. 'Goldie' isn't exactly what comes to mind when you look at me. I just love irony. The idea of being the opposite of what people expect is ingrained in my psyche. The first time I heard Charlotte say it, I loved it. And yes, in case you're wondering, this *is* my natural hair color."

Goldie pauses and we all look at Shorty.

"Well, my name is Rebel," she begins. Her words are drawn out slow and smooth, like honey. "My story isn't quite as crazy as theirs. No car wrecks, no rescues, none of that. We met just this side of Kinston, where I had taken over an abandoned farm.

"Anyway, there I was standing by the road at the end of my driveway and here comes this humongous RV camper as big as a Greyhound bus. Now, I hadn't seen anybody since I came to at my house nine months before. I know they've spotted me, but I'm not too worried because I have my handgun and my shotgun and I know how to use 'em. Well, they get to where I'm standing...air brakes hissing and dust flying...and Charlotte here sticks her head out the driver's side window and says, 'You know the way to New Bern? We're lost.' I knew right then that these were my people because I'm forever getting lost when I drive somewhere."

"Three times just on the trip here," Goldie says. "I guess none of us are very good at reading maps. We are definitely children of the electronic age."

"So, why 'Rebel?'" Roxie asks. She looks stronger now, but her face is still swollen. "Is it a Southern thing?"

"Oh, heck no. Nothing like that. I chose Rebel because when I came to and looked at myself in the mirror for the first time, I thought I was looking at Rebel Wilson. You know, the actress. Shorter, maybe, but the same hair, cheeks and eyes. A perfect match face-wise, at least the way she looks these days. So, I had already started calling myself Rebel before I met these two. I love her movies!"

Roxie and I look at each other, struggling with the same question.

"But, can you sing?" Roxie asks. "You know, like in Pitch Perfect?"

"Charlotte and Goldie snicker at that.

"I don't know..." Rebel says, her voice trailing off as if wondering why she hadn't thought of that herself. "But I do know this! I'm at least one of the best five singers in the known world!"

All of us laugh this time and the tension that had been hanging over us earlier disappears. We're starting to bond, and that's a good thing.

"So, here we are," Charlotte says, wrapping up the introductions. "We got lost again and, to tell the truth, we're not sure where we are now. We've gotten lost so many times, we've started calling ourselves The Lost Girls."

CHAPTER TWENTY-FOUR

Lonely Hunter

"Rebel was keeping watch at the front of the grocery store while Goldie and I loaded up the motorcoach with a few staples and canned foods," Charlotte says, firelight reflecting off her dark face. "We haven't been together long. But we came up with the idea to park the bus out of sight behind the building...so nobody would see us before we saw them. Not that we expected to find anybody else. But we do it every time we make a stop. Better safe than sorry."

"When y'all drove into the parking lot, I gave the alert and we watched you go into the drugstore," Rebel says, tossing a log into the metal fire bowl Roxie and I set up behind the house back in the spring. Sparks swirl above the flames for a moment, then die out in mid-air. "I can whistle real loud. I guess you can say it's our standard operating procedure. S-O-P. That's a thing, right?"

"Of course, you guys are the first people we've seen," Goldie says, "and boy, are we glad to find you. We haven't seen *anybody* out there."

"The thing is," Charlotte says, "even though we created a plan for approaching new people, we didn't work out what to do after first contact. It's kind of stupid but, like Rebel said, we haven't been together long. And to be honest, it didn't seem likely we would find anyone else."

"What about the rest of the state?" I ask. Tonka, worn out from retrieving his favorite toy Roxie had thrown for him, jumps into my lap and rests his head on the wide arm of my Adirondack chair.

"Yeah..." Charlotte says, weighing her words before answering. "Well, the city of Charlotte has a population of about a million people. I spent months looking for other people but didn't find anyone. The last few weeks before I left, I would set a house on fire every few days at noon, hoping someone would spot it and check it out."

"Wow!" Roxie says. "How cool is that? Wish I had thought of it."

A chorus of laughs and giggles ripples through our little group before Charlotte continues.

"I burned down a house about every three days. I would throw containers of motor oil on the fire so it would make a lot of black smoke. After burning one down, I'd wait a day to see if anyone showed up. On the third day, I would move to a different section of the city and try again."

"When we go to new places, we put speakers on the outside of the truck or boat and play music real loud," I say. "I guess either way works."

"But hers is way more fun," Roxie says. We all laugh again, but not quite as loud. It's hard to tell if she's trying to be funny or maybe liking the idea of setting fires a bit too much.

"Living in a vast city with hundreds of thousands of empty houses and buildings is weird," Charlotte continues. "It was creeping me out. But if I was going to leave, I figured I'd go to places like Greensboro and Raleigh to look for other people. You know, the greater the population, the better the odds of finding someone."

"Why not go south?" I ask.

"Honestly, I don't know. I felt drawn to come this way. Something inside me kept saying, go east. So here I am."

"I was considering going west to look for people. But if you didn't find anybody, I don't see any point to it now."

"I thought I did, once," she says. "After spending about a month in the Greensboro area burning down houses every three days, I moved on to Durham and

Chapel Hill. But as I was getting close to Raleigh, I saw smoke in the distance. I thought it was somebody using the same strategy. Only, when I found the place, I realized it wasn't smoke. It was a steam cloud from a nuclear power plant. The darn thing is still running by itself."

"Holy smoke," Goldie says, oblivious to the ill timing of her unintended pun, "you didn't tell us about the nuke plant. If nobody is running it, won't it explode or melt down or something?"

"I don't know," Charlotte says. "Maybe it will. I guess we'll know if it blows up. We'll be able to see the mushroom cloud from here."

"Not funny," Rebel says. "Ain't no way I want to be turned into a crispy critter."

Everybody laughs, more out of tension than the weird mental picture created by the vivid alliteration.

"I don't think you'll have to worry about burning up this far away," Roxie says, further establishing herself as the expert on all things fire related. "You'll just be easier to find at night."

"What do ya mean?" Rebel says.

"We'll all be radioactive...you'll glow in the dark."

Roxie snorts at her dark joke while everybody else groans with exaggerated annoyance.

"I've never seen this side of you before," I say to Roxie.

"I didn't know I had a side like this," she says. "Maybe I just needed an audience."

Roxie pokes at the fire with a hoe and everyone turns quiet, processing the stories we've shared.

Once we felt sure the so-called Lost Girls weren't a threat, Roxie and I invited them to follow us back to the house in their motorcoach. It's gigantic, just as Rebel said. It's so big it almost couldn't fit through the sections Roxie and I had cut out of the trees blocking the road. But we made it OK. Well...except for the turkey incident.

Roxie was leading the way in the truck while I rode in the coach with the girls, providing a running narrative of the area as we drove along. As usual, we passed by hundreds of deer feeding along the road and even a few bears. The three girls weren't impressed.

"It's been like this almost everywhere I've been," Charlotte had said, sitting behind the steering wheel. "Deer, bear, coyotes, bobcats...you name it. Nature is really taking over."

"I wouldn't want to be anywhere near Asheboro," Goldie said.

"Why's that?" I asked. "What's in Asheboro?"

"The state zoo. Think about it. Lions, elephants, rhinos, baboons, grizzlies, wolves and freaking gorillas!"

"Look out!" Rebel yelled. Charlotte slammed on the brakes.

Looking out the windshield, I saw Roxie struggling to keep the truck on the road, stopping just before going into the ditch. We sat frozen for a moment, waiting to see if the tarp over the beehive was going to stay secure or if the bees would come flooding out. But everything stayed in place.

"What happened?" I asked, fumbling with the door. The handle was more like something on an airplane than a car.

"She hit an animal," Rebel said. "An enormous bird of some kind. Look, there's more of them."

We all piled out of the coach and joined Roxie, who was standing outside the truck's cab. A hoard of wild turkeys streamed around the truck and motorcoach, oblivious to our presence. They just wanted to move from one side of the road to the other. They had no fear of us at all.

"I tried to swerve around it," Roxie said. "I didn't want to slam on brakes and make you guys rear end me. Not sure what kind of stopping distance that thing has. Anyway, the turkey flew up at the last moment. Instead of zigging away, it zagged right into me. Stupid bird."

"Is it dead?" I asked.

"Oh, it's deceased alright," Goldie said, standing in front of the truck. She held up a humongous, undeniably and reliably dead gobbler by the neck.

"That *is* a big bird," Charlotte said, impressed.

"You know what I think it is?" Rebel asks. "Supper!"

"Oh, yeah!" Roxie says, "I haven't had turkey in...well...I don't know how long. But judging by the dance the taste buds in my mouth are doing now, I know I like it."

"Why not?" I said. "In fact, given the circumstances, I think we should have a feast tonight. Celebrate our coming together."

"Yeah!" Goldie said. "That's a phenomenal idea!"

"Nothing says 'feast' like roasted roadkill," Rebel said, and we all laughed. This girl's sense of humor is off the chart.

Goldie laid the turkey next to the beehive in the back of the truck and we resumed our trip. Once we were home, Rebel volunteered to pluck and dress the turkey while the rest of us picked out our favorite dishes...or the closest things to them we could concoct...and prepared the best meal any of us had had since the storm. And, thanks to the snap beans Roxie and I had already harvested, the green bean casserole I made with powdered milk and soup turned out fantastic!

As we ate, we compared notes and learned more about each other. Because we all had made-up names, it wasn't surprising to discover each of us had suffered a traumatic head injury and memory loss. Charlotte had found herself at the bottom of a hotel stairwell after the storm. Goldie had crawled out of a wrecked car. Rebel had come to in an open field with no clue how she had been injured...just that her head was bleeding and she was suffering a terrific headache. Their loss of memory worked the same as mine...selectively. We still had base educational knowledge and possessed advanced skills, but no memories of our childhoods, parents, ages...or anything about who we are as individuals.

Each of us discovered everyone was gone but believed they would come back. When they didn't, each of us searched for other people, only to find small piles of sand and salt. Since coming together, we've focused on surviving.

But what we didn't say was even more important. Our suspicions about what happened to people and why we had survived remained unspoken, hanging in the shadows, refusing to make themselves known. For now, they were unwelcomed guests and none of us dared invite them to the table because we feared them. The classic, "let's leave well enough alone."

After stuffing ourselves, the Lost Girls cleaned up while Roxie and I gathered wood for the fire bowl in the backyard. By the time the girls finished, it was almost dark, and the fire was burning strong. With a rotation of light jazz playing softly in the background, our conversation lulls and we become lost in our own thoughts for a few moments.

"You two have a great place here," Charlotte says, breaking the spell. "Solar power, well water, the vegetable gardens, the boat...it makes me kind of nostalgic for home...even though I don't know what my home was like."

"You guys are welcome to stay here," I say. Tonka nudges me and I resume scratching his head. "For the time being, you can stay in the house with us or in the motorcoach, whatever works best for you. If you stay, we can go to the solar farm nearby, pick up a few solar panels and wire them to one of the houses across the street. That way, you'll all have plenty of room."

"Go back to the other thing you said," Roxie says. "The thing about not remembering what your home was like."

"Yeah," Charlotte says. "What about it?"

"Isn't it strange how none of us have memories from before the storm? And, heck, according to you and Goldie, the hurricane hardly affected Goldsboro. And the city of Charlotte, not at all. So, whatever took place didn't happen because of the storm. You know what I mean? The hurricane here didn't make people in California disappear. The storm was just a coincidence."

"So it would seem," Goldie says, still staring into the flames. "I think the fact we all suffered head injuries has something to do with why we survived...like maybe it somehow blocked whatever got the others."

"I've had the same thoughts," I say. "I sort of suspected it when Roxie told me about her injury. And now, you guys... It's too much of a coincidence for it to have happened to all five of us."

"And the piles of sand and salt," Roxie says, taking the baton, "we all know what those are, right?"

"It's what's left of all the people," Rebel says, her voice devoid of emotion. "It has to be. We know those piles exist all the way from here to Charlotte, and I don't see any reason to believe they aren't everywhere on the planet."

No one says anything or even nods their head in agreement. It's group denial. As long as no one agrees, maybe it won't be true. But we all know better.

"So...I have a question," Charlotte says, changing the subject. "Where are the boy survivors? Shouldn't there be a few guys who suffered head injuries still alive? I know the odds are low, but it happened to the five of us. Statistically, shouldn't four, five or six guys have made it, too?"

"I hadn't thought of that," Goldie says, "but you're right. Where *are* the boys? Did we survive because we don't have a Y chromosome and they do?"

"Whoa!" Rebel says. "You guys are freaking me out. I'm not looking to be in a relationship or anything, but no way do I want to be a nun the rest of my life...not that there's anything wrong with that...if that's what you want. But for me? Nope! No! No way, José! I want a boyfriend someday."

Rebel's statement is the exclamation point to our dour mood...if a pall can have an exclamation point. Roxie pulls her legs up to her chest and wraps her arms around her knees. Rebel, who's sharing a chair with Goldie, rests her cheek on the red-haired girl's shoulder. Charlotte leans forward, placing one elbow on the chair's arm and rests her cheek on her hand. Only the sounds from a massive chorus of tree frogs and the crackling fire disturb the silence.

Our melancholy is palpable and smothering. Each of us is lost in our thoughts, imagining the hopelessness of an existence without natural fulfillment...not just for ourselves, but for all humanity. From somewhere, deep down in my suppressed memories, a poem comes to mind. I recite it without considering its meaning.

"O never a green leaf whispers,
"Where the green-gold branches swing.
"O never a song I hear now,
"Where one was wont to sing.
"Here in the heart of summer,
"Sweet is life to me still,
"But my heart is a lonely hunter...
"That hunts on a lonely hill."

My voice trails off as I recite the last line, ending in a whisper. No one speaks, and for a moment I wonder if I had thought the words.

"That was beautiful," Roxie says at last. "What is it?

"It's the last stanza from a poem titled The Lonely Hunter. Don't ask me how I know. It's about a young woman whose fiancé has died young, and she wanders the countryside, forever lamenting his death...and the death of her heart."

"But you haven't lost anyone. Or, if you have, you have no way of knowing."

"Yes...I have," I say. Tears well in my eyes and I blink them back. "And so have you. All of us have. If no one else is left on earth, then not only have we lost the people we would have fallen in love with, once we are gone, humanity will be gone. Love will disappear forever."

CHAPTER TWENTY-FIVE

Odd Girl Out

The new day brings new perspective. Determined to leave last night's low behind, I draw on the blessings we share to reset my mental outlook to positive. We are five girls...almost women...who have survived a great cataclysm of unknown origin. By combining our talents, we *will* continue to endure. We will face the future together, come what may. Fate will take care of fate. Everything else is up to us.

With my attitude properly adjusted, we hit the ground running. *I don't know the origin of this idiom, but it sounds good.* Together, we go out in the truck with a trailer attached and collect the solar panels we need. Then we hook them up to the house across the street. We also salvage some cisterns from a home-and-garden store to collect rainwater from the roof and connect a pump so the girls can have running water inside the house.

In between, we finish harvesting vegetables from the garden and store them as best we can to preserve them. The desktop computer is a big help with this, and we learn a lot. Before the end of the next growing season, we plan to gather the kitchen gadgets and containers we need to can fruits and vegetables, which...as it turns out...doesn't involve cans. The prepared foods are put into jars and sealed with lids. Seems to me it should be called jarring, but what do I know?

In addition to our little journey to retrieve the solar panels, we take several excursions to the Kinston area. Rebel, having lived in the area, knows of several farms with livestock foraging on their own. Over the next few days, we accumulate a nice assortment of goats, chickens, rabbits and even a llama. Of course, we need the llama to protect the other animals from predators. It was either a llama or a donkey. So, we went with the llama because...well...it's a freaking llama! Who doesn't love llamas?

Our work brings us closer together, and we are becoming a family. And like any family, we have our individual talents, likes, and dislikes. Charlotte is exactly what she seemed to be from the beginning...cool, competent, fearless, bossy and demanding. We butt heads...a lot. It wouldn't be wrong to say we're both alpha females, but it would be a disservice to the other girls. We're all alphas to varying degrees and in different ways.

Despite the daily battle to exert our wills, Charlotte and I respect each other. She has a knack for building and planning. Which of course, I don't. Our skills complement each other well.

Goldie is liquid glue...she seeps into any cracks that form between us, binds us together, and never waivers during a fray. Rebel has become her best friend and they do almost everything together. She also has crazy math and computer skills. Since learning we have a functioning desktop computer in the upstairs office, Goldie spends hours exploring the files and making notes of where to find the information we need most.

Rebel is the sweetie nobody can ever be mad at. She is all heart and love, and it shows most when she works with animals. They are her children, and when we lose one, she's a wreck. She also has a wicked sense of humor and never fails to make us laugh. Even better, she has no qualms about laughing at herself. She's authentic in every way.

Roxie, the girl who almost lost her life in a kayak while trying to find me, is my best friend, next to Tonka. Her most dominant personality trait is her spirituality, her connection to the living world. Before the Great Vanishing, people might have called her a pantheist...a person who believes a single spirit exists in all living things. That we are all connected by that spirit. Sort of like The Force in the Star Wars saga, but real, and not limited to a group of lightsaber-wielding space monks.

In a weird way, her spirituality was the reason she almost gave up on life. Until we found each other, she had no one to share her soul with. Living in a spiritual vacuum just didn't work for her.

Of the five of us, she's the only one I worry about. Her blackouts are becoming more frequent. They are manageable and her mood changes still alert me to when one might occur. But I fear this won't last much longer because the time between the mood shifts and spells is becoming shorter. I hide my concern as best I can and have coached the other girls to do the same, but my inability to help her makes me sick. I hate feeling inadequate, especially when I know there must be a procedure to treat her problem. After spending countless hours on the computer, however, the only possible remedy I've found is far too dangerous. She needs a doctor. She needs a brain surgeon.

One thing all four of them...all five of us...have in common is, we are incredibly intelligent. I never talk about myself this way. I disdain conceit. But in attempting to understand why we survive while most people did not, I must consider every trait we share. We're all teenage girls, forced by extreme circumstances to be as women. Each of us have distinct and well-developed talents. We all suffered a head injury. And our IQs are off the chart. We share too many commonalities to believe we are alive by coincidence. But if an outside force influenced our survival, I can't imagine what it might have been. I doubt we will never know the truth.

And then there's Tonka...the everything dog. Did I say dog? Shame on me. Tonka is the most beloved member of our little family. He is everyone's buddy, and he never disappoints. He is fearless, confident and loves going on excursions. His two favorite forms of fun are fetching his favorite green squeaky toy and herding. Yeah, it's weird to see a breed created to hunt rodents herding goats, but he loves it. Chasing them around the pen gives him an outlet for his hunting instincts and provides us with entertainment. He's also smart enough to leave the llama alone. Llamas can be downright mean when they want to be.

Tonka doesn't belong to me...I belong to him. He loves the other girls too, but he always comes to my side if there's even a hint of danger. And when it's time to turn in for the night, it's on my bed he sleeps. It's impossible to know what my life was like before the storm, but I can't imagine how it could have been better without Tonka by my side.

He loves being on the water. Or maybe he just loves not being left behind when we go sailing. Today is no exception. He leads the way to the dock with us following close behind. I'm pulling the wagon loaded with inner tubes. It's late September, the air is cool, but the water is still warm, and we're taking a day off from our work. We've earned it.

"I'll pilot the boat this time," Charlotte says. The words are a declaration rather than a request.

All the girls are well-versed on how to handle the boat, whether under sail or when using the engine. So, competence isn't an issue. And while I've learned to ignore Charlotte's abrasive manner most of the time, it can still be grating.

"Aren't you the person who almost ran into the channel marker?" Goldie teases as she steps into the boat. "I mean, the river is as wide as the Grand Canyon, and you somehow almost manage to kill us running into the only obstruction within miles. How does that happen?"

"It happens when the helmsman is stuffing her face with jerky, chips, peanuts and other junk food instead of paying attention," Rebel says, piling on.

"HA. HA. HA." Charlotte says with a sarcastic laugh. "We were all eating. It was lunchtime, and the boat was drifting. *Nobody* was paying attention, and *nobody* was at the helm."

"Oh, but you were supposed to be," Roxie says, handing Goldie one of the inner tubes. "I remember it well...what was it you said? Oh, yeah, 'I'll show you girls how to make a sailboat fly across the water and jibe on a dime. Watch and learn.' Did I get that right, Char?"

"Very funny," Charlotte says. "That was *before* we dropped sail to take a break. Funny how you forget the important part."

"OK, girls…" I say, using my most motherly voice. "Y'all best behave, or I'll have to send you to your rooms and ground you."

Everybody stares at me a moment and then laughs.

"Please don't ground me, mom," Roxie pleads. "You know the big dance is tomorrow night and I've just *got* to go. What will all the other kids say?"

We laugh, but it's a hollow cliché. We understand the concepts of being grounded and going to the prom, but none of us have memories of doing these things. It's sad, but it's who we are.

"Alright," I say, passing Tonka over to Roxie and climbing aboard Icebreaker, "Char, you take the helm. But remember, this is a pleasure trip. We just need to put some distance between us and the riverbanks. Away from snapping turtles and alligators."

"And the water moccasins!" Rebel interrupts.

"Yes, and the snakes," I continue. "We won't even need to raise sail. Just putter out to open water using the engine."

"That's a good thing," Charlotte says. "I'd hate for the sail to catch a big gust of wind and have the boom knock certain people off the boat for the alligators to eat."

"You just try it and see what happens," Goldie says.

And so it goes for the next few hours, five girls engaging in friendly banter while enjoying the warm water and drifting on the inner tubes. Even Tonka, wearing his oh-so-cute doggie life vest, joins in, paddling around after his toy and barking for attention when ignored too long. The MP-3 is playing "Pontoon" by Little Big Town, the perfect background music for a perfect day on the water.

"I could do this forever," Charlotte says as we float in our inner tubes, soaking up the sun. "We've been working and training so hard, I forgot what it was like to just do nothing."

"True that," I say. The other three girls are taking turns diving off the bow of the boat with a playlist of tunes Rebel put together, blasting through the Bluetooth speaker. Tonka watches them from the helmsman's seat, taking a break from the fun. "We've accomplished a lot, and we still have tons to do, but I think we are in a good place. Once we gather enough wood to burn for the winter, we'll have some real down time."

"Please, stop! No more talk about work we have to do. Enjoy the moment!"

"You're right," I sigh. "Sometimes it's hard to turn my brain off, you know. We have so much we need to learn. One of us needs to be researching medicine. You or me, maybe. And we need a veterinarian...that has Rebel's name written all over it. And then–"

"Oh my god!" Charlotte says, kicking the side of my inner tube. "You're doing it again! Stop!"

"Wait!" I say, not sure whether to believe what I'd just seen. "Do that again."

"Do what again? Kick you?"

"No! Lift your foot out of the water."

Her facial expression says, "Nope, I'm not falling for that trick."

"Seriously. Lift your right leg. I'm not going to do anything."

She raises her leg out of the water while keeping a wary eye on me.

"What the heck is that?" I say, pointing to her ankle. It's a symbol of some kind. Like a stick figure with an oblong head, its arms stretched to either side on a horizontal plane.

"Uh...a tattoo," she says, like I'm the dumbest person in the world.

"A tattoo of what?"

"An ankh. You know, the Egyptian symbol for life. You haven't noticed it until now?"

"No. I've never seen you when you weren't wearing your hiking boots and socks. There's no way I could have seen it."

"Yeah, that makes sense. It's nothing special. I have no memory of why or when I got it. It seemed pretty new when I came to from being knocked out. I guess it has something to do with my heritage. Don't you think I look a lot like Nefertari...dark eyes, brown skin, black hair, thin face, small nose...a classic beauty. I would have said Cleopatra, but Elizabeth Taylor ruined that comparison. Besides, Cleopatra was Greek."

"You know who else has a tattoo?" I say. "Roxie. She has a tattoo on her ankle...in the exact same spot."

Charlotte shoots me with a stunned look. It's the first time I've ever seen her at a loss for words.

"Goldie has one too," she says at last. "I saw it the first time we met. We had gotten muddy and needed to hose our shoes and feet off before getting back in the motorcoach. I didn't say anything because we were in a rush. Then I forgot."

"On the ankle, in the same place?"

"Yeah!"

"What is it?"

"I don't know. Like I said, I forgot and never asked about it."

"Goldie!" I say, catching her just before jumping off the bow to do a cannonball. Charlotte and I hand-paddle closer to the sailboat.

"Yeah, what is it?"

"The tattoo on your leg...can I see it?"

"Sure," she says as we catch hold of the stern ladder and climb out of the water.

We meet at the cabin entryway and she holds her right leg out like she's a foot model or something. The tattoo is an endless ribbon woven into a collection of small diamond shapes on both the outside edges and the inside holes.

"It's a Mongolian Ulzii," she says, "the symbol of eternal happiness and life. I'm sure it's connected to my heritage somehow. There are many Mongolians with red hair, you know."

"And like you said, it's in the exact same spot as yours and Roxie's," I say to Charlotte.

"OK, this is weird," Roxie says, placing her foot next to Goldie's, showing the sun symbol on her ankle. Everyone has stopped what they were doing and come together in a circle. "Mine is a Zia. Or to be more accurate…a sun symbol of the Native American people of New Mexico named the Zia. The four sets of four lines extending from the circle in the middle are said to represent different aspects of Zia culture, the sacred obligations of their society. It's basically a life symbol. But don't ask me how I know all this stuff."

"Oh my god, y'all," Rebel says, sliding her foot up to the others. "I have one, too. This is too much!"

We all stare at the tattoo on her ankle. Hers is an interwoven shape, too. But instead of a ribbon, the lines look more like a loosely knotted rope forming three football-shaped spheroids.

"It's called a triquetra. It represents various aspects of Celtic culture, sort of like what Roxie said about the Zia. Some people say it represents the Holy Trinity…you know…the Father, the Son, and the Holy Ghost. But it was used by the Pagans before the Christians adopted it. Some say it signifies the Triple Moon Goddess, which comprises the maiden, the mother and the crone, or wisdom, and is connected to female fertility. So…yeah…it's a life symbol too, any way you look at it."

"And you know that, how?" I ask.

"Not a clue. It just came to me when I stuck my foot out."

That I haven't entered my foot into the ring becomes more conspicuous with each passing second. I'm sure they're all looking at me, waiting for the big reveal. Surrendering to the inevitable, I brace myself and look up to see four expectant faces staring at me. *My* face turns red.

"I don't have a tattoo," I say, as though announcing I'm a leper. "Not on my ankle. Not anywhere."

"Well, don't feel guilty about it," Roxie says, seeing my discomfort. "I know what my tattoo symbolizes, but I have no idea when I got it or why. I remember it seemed new the first time I saw it after the hurricane. It itched a little. But I didn't think about it at all. Too much other stuff going on."

"Same here," Goldie says. Rebel and Charlotte nod their heads in agreement.

"But it's got to mean something. It's too much of a coincidence the four of you...separated by hundreds of miles and never having met each other...all got tats right before the weird apocalypse, and they all symbolize life in some way."

"Maybe we did know each other," Roxie says. "Without our before-time memories, there's no way to know. Maybe you were part of the group, too. Maybe you were going to get a tattoo, but couldn't because you were out sailing or something."

"Maybe," I say, shaking my head, "but it doesn't seem likely."

"OK then, Madame Currie," Charlotte says, "what do you think is the reason? You think we should kick you off our planet because we have tats and you don't?"

"I have another theory," Roxie says. Her eyes are fixed on a spot in the distance, trying to nail down the thought before saying it. "Maybe we were marked for something related to the disappearance. Maybe something good, maybe something bad. Who knows? And maybe you were supposed to be tattooed just like us, but you didn't get yours because you were out on the ocean in your boat."

"Or..." I say, my words coming out low and ragged, "maybe I was supposed to disappear. Maybe I'm not supposed to be alive."

CHAPTER TWENTY-SIX

Shooting Stars

"Want me to throw another log on?" Rebel says to no one in particular. "I'm colder than a wet Wildling at Winterfell. I hate being cold. It hurts me to my bones."

"Wildlings don't live in Winterfell," Goldie says with mock indignation. "Wildlings live in the North. Places like the Haunted Forest and Frozen Shore."

Rebel curls her lip into a sneer and strikes her best woman warrior pose...which is pretty menacing thanks to the glowing red embers in the fire bowl.

"You know nothing, Jon Snow. I was going for alliteration, not accuracy. Ygritte is not amused."

We all groan, then laugh despite ourselves. Since watching Game of Thrones several weeks ago on the computer, we've had lots of fun inserting lines from the series into our conversations.

"If anybody says, 'Winter is coming,' you'll be banished to the Night's Watch for life," Charlotte says, and everyone groans again.

"Too late!" Goldie says, pointing her finger northward. "You've violated your own edict!" "Off to The Wall with you!"

"Poor Charlotte!" I say, joining in. "She's going to freeze her buns off! It's too bad we're all going to miss it. You know? Because, just like the end of Thrones, it's so dark, nobody can see what's happening."

"No kidding!" Roxie says. "The most epic battle in the history of cinema...and nobody could see it! What were they thinking?"

For the millionth time, we digress into a debate about everything wrong with the show's conclusion and how we would have made it better. And as usual, the thing we disagree on most is whether it should be Sansa, Arya, or Daenerys Targaryen who becomes Ruler of the World instead of Bran the Boring. It's a weird conversation to have on Christmas Eve, but it's great fun.

"OK," Rebel says. "I never got an answer. Do we keep the fire going or not?"

"Nah," I say, shoving my hands into the pockets of my down-filled coat. "I think it's time to let it die out."

Tonka, who's sitting on my lap chewing on his favorite toy, gives me his hollow "don't annoy me" growl. He doesn't appreciate being disturbed.

"How about we sing one last Christmas carol?" Roxie says, though her tone suggests her heart isn't in it.

"Nooo!" Charlotte says. "I mean, it was fun for a while. Now...not so much."

"Char's right," Goldie says. "It was a good thing to do after such a scrumptious feast, and it being the night before Christmas and all. But the more we sang, the less fun it was. There's no context to it."

"What do you mean?" I ask, though I know the answer. I need her to give voice to what we are all thinking.

"We sing the songs because, somehow, we still know the words and the tunes. It's tradition. But we have no memories of past holidays. No memories of being with family or opening presents or drinking gross eggnog. None of those things. Heck, we don't even know if any of us are Christians."

"You don't have to be a Christian to enjoy Christmas," Rebel says.

"I know," Goldie shoots back, frustration honing an edge on her words. "But I don't even know *how* I know! This selective memory disorder is so random. I might be a Christian. I might be a Buddhist. If we're going by my tattoo, I might be an Abijiya. Why can't I remember? I want to remember!"

"What's an Abijiya?" Rebel asks.

"It's a Mongolian female shaman. And see, I don't even know why I know *that*! It drives me nuts!"

It was Goldie who discovered it was almost Christmas. She was researching husbandry on the computer and noticed the timestamp at the bottom of the screen. It was December twenty-second...three days before Christmas. She had been all excited and suggested we celebrate. Everyone else thought it was a great idea, too. A chance to have some fun!

Charlotte...the big city girl turned big-time hunter...went out the next day with her rifle and brought back a small boar. Or a feral pig. It's hard to tell the difference when they're small. But it was perfect for smoking on the pig cooker we commandeered for grilling large game.

While Charlotte is the only one who's taken up hunting, we don't balk at eating fresh meat. It's solid protein. It might not have been part of our diet back in the before time, but we need it now. Our bodies demand it. I guess when humans revert to their base nature, meat becomes a necessity.

Besides, game is so abundant. It would be crazy not to take advantage of food that delivers itself to your door. There's nothing like an apocalypse to make everyone a realist. And we understand we can't depend on canned foods and dry staples forever. Sure, the processed stuff will last for years. But it's already losing its taste and nutritional value. Not to mention some of it looks really nasty.

"Look at the stars," Rebel says, breaking the silence hanging over our little clan. "The air is so crisp and clear, it's as though you could reach out and touch them. It's like a giant swallowed a keg of diamonds and threw up all over the sky."

"What?" Goldie says, laughing. "A giant throwing up diamonds. That's ridiculous. How do you come up with this stuff?

"Thanks for the mental image," Charlotte says. "Now I need a barf bag. You do realize puking and diamonds don't go together, right?"

"I can't help it!" Rebel says. "Sometimes my mouth engages before my brain. But it is beautiful, right?"

"Oooo…look," Roxie says, coming to Rebel's rescue. "There's Betelgeuse and Rigel, and in between is Orion's Belt. See it?"

"Yes!" I say, excited to discover someone else in our group knows the stars. "I didn't know you were familiar with astrology and constellations."

"I didn't either!" she laughs. "Not until just now. Hey, let's go down to the dock and see what other stars we can identify."

"You guys have a grand time," Charlotte says as Rebel lets out a long yawn. "I'm ready for bed."

"I'm done too," Goldie says. "I'm going to put out the fire and turn in."

"Sounds like a plan to me," Rebel chimes in, yawning again.

Roxie and I head to the dock, leaving the Lost Girls to gather their blankets and douse the fire. The stars are so bright we have no trouble seeing our way down the pier. Tonka follows, carrying his green toy. It's a perfect night for stargazing.

Just before reaching the dock, a pair of ducks take to the air in a flurry of flapping wings, blaring quacks of alarm. Out of reflex, Roxie and I reach for our sidearms, but stop when we realize there's no threat. At the same moment, Tonka drops his toy and barks. Too late, I see the green, dumbbell-shaped toy roll off the boarded walkway, landing in the marsh with a plop. Tonka looks over the edge of the planks, staring at his favorite toy laying in mud.

"It's a good thing we weren't on the dock yet," I say to my Westie friend. "If your toy had fallen into the creek, we'd never get it back."

Roxie lies along the edge of the pier, reaching down to grab it. She stretches as far as she can, then teeters precariously. I grab the end of her coat and pull her back just before she goes over the edge.

"It's OK," I say. "The pier's too high off the ground. We'll get it tomorrow with a landing net or something. It's not like it's going anywhere. Come on. Let's see how many constellations we can name."

Leaning back in the chairs we keep on the dock, Roxie and I wonder at the billions of suns we call stars. There's no moon, there's no ambient light, there's no pollution of any kind anymore. We're able to see the stars the way our ancestors had for thousands of years...perfect and unobstructed. Roxie sees a meteor burn out in the atmosphere, points to it and says...

> *"Sister, if seas part us, do you not consider me?*
> *Tell them I sang the ancient psalms at dusk*
> *inside the wire and strong men wept. Turn thee*
> *unto me with mercy, for I am desolate and lost."*

"What was that?" I ask in a stunned whisper.

"From a poem," she says, trying to pull the details from her repressed memory. "It's the last stanza from Shooting Stars. It's a poem about the Holocaust. The rest of the poem is even darker."

"Do you think you're Jewish?" I ask, unable to think of anything else to say.

"No," she says without hesitating. The quickness of her answer...an unfiltered recollection from her long-term memory...makes me believe she must be right. "But if I am Native American, it's a poem my people would relate to. And now, those of us who remain can understand it, too...because we've survived an apocalypse...which is our own holocaust."

I do understand. But what disturbs me isn't what the words recount, but what they might portend. The idea of us being parted tears at my heart, and I pray it will never happen.

"Oh my god, look!" she says, pointing to the southwest, just above the horizon. "That star! It's moving across the sky! And it's twinkling."

"No…" I say, waiting until I see enough to confirm my suspicion. My next words come out as a whisper. "It's not a star. It's a satellite. A man-made object."

"But…there's no way. How could a small satellite reflect so much light?"

"Because it's not a communication satellite," I say. "It's a much bigger satellite. It's the space station."

We watch in awe as the blinking light traverses the horizon at 17,000 miles an hour. It's a stark reminder of what humanity had achieved and what we've lost. It's hard to imagine our species ever returning to such a pinnacle of technological achievement. Even more depressing, at this moment, it's hard to imagine humanity will even survive.

"Roxie…" I whisper as the satellite disappears behind the southern horizon.

"Yeah?"

"Did you notice anything peculiar about the blinking?"

"Not really. What do you mean?"

"I think it was Morse code. I'm not kidding."

"No way!"

"Way! I didn't notice it at first. But when I replay it in my mind, I'm sure it blinked three quick flashes for S and three longs for O. It wasn't visible long enough to see more, but that's how S-O-S begins!"

"Whoa…" Roxie says. "Do you know what this means?"

"Yeah," I say, grateful we had come to the same conclusion. "There might still be people up there! You know? Astronauts!"

It's a stunning revelation. Yet, one so obvious it makes me wonder why we hadn't thought of it before.

"What if..." she says, continuing the theory. "What if the thing that reduced humans to piles of silica didn't affect the space station's crew...and they're still up there, waiting?"

"That would be horrible," I say. My throat is constricted so tight it feels like I've swallowed a tennis ball. "I wish we could communicate with them...you know...find out if they're still alive. There's no way we can help them, but they might know what happened."

"But...there is a way," she says. "The base at Cherry Point...they have all kinds of sophisticated communication equipment. It's a Marine Corps air station, right? I remember seeing a building surrounded by a zillion antennas. It was on a street with a weird name. Cryogenics Road! Yeah, that's it. They must have radios with the right frequency to call the space station."

"Brilliant!" It's a simple concept, but it rings true and fills me with an excitement I haven't felt in a long time. "We'll tell the others first thing tomorrow and go to Cherry Point A-S-A-P! What do you think?"

"I think it's a phenomenal idea!" Roxie says, the excitement in her voice matching mine. "I don't think I'll be able to sleep tonight!"

"Me either," I say, rising from the chair. "But we have to try. There's lots we have to do tomorrow to get ready. We need to be rested and ready to go. We should be ready to sail to Cherry Point the day after tomorrow if the weather's good."

"Yes!" Roxie says, jumping from her chair to give me a hug. "I agree! It'll sort of be like a homecoming for me. And, if we connect with people who know what happened...so much the better!"

"You know," I say, "going to Cherry Point to look for radio equipment was totally your idea. I never would have thought of it."

"Oh...thanks, but you deserve credit, too. I mean, you're the one who noticed the S-O-S thing."

We remain quiet for a moment, the possibilities of what the next days might bring overloading our imaginations.

"Roxie..." I say at last. "There's something else I want to say before we go in."

"Yeah?"

"It's after midnight...Merry Christmas!"

CHAPTER TWENTY-SEVEN

The Fog

Roxie was right about not sleeping. The possibility of finding other people has blasted my imagination into warp speed…no pun intended. There are so many things to consider. The idea people were on the space station when everyone on earth disappeared is a certainty. Whether they were still alive was another question.

Did they survive the Great Vanishing? Were they able to leave the space station and return to earth? If so, where are they now? If not, did they have enough air, water and food to have survived the past fifteen months?

I've been lying in the bed for an hour with these questions swirling in my head like a fidget spinner. Totally amped up and wide awake, I roll out of bed to look out the window overlooking the marsh. Resting in his usual place at the foot of the mattress, Tonka lifts his head to see what I'm doing. Satisfied I'm not going anywhere, he closes his eyes and falls asleep again.

The crystal-clear conditions and brightness of the stars allowing us to spot the space station haven't changed. I can see everything in the backyard, the fire bowl, the chairs, the landscape features. The cattails begin at the backyard's edge and continue all the way to the creek. The pier blazing a path through the cattails and over the marsh. I can even see the outline of Icebreaker tethered securely to the dock.

It's a peaceful, surreal scene, giving me hope for the future and appreciation for how awesome our little homestead is. As excited as I am for what we might find in the days ahead, I know we're going to be all right...no matter what.

My gaze carries beyond the creek out to the river, and I see that this perfect winter night is almost done. While a part of me is disappointed, I'm a realist. All good things...as they say...must come to an end.

A bank of mist is inching toward the house, blanking out the stars and the landscape behind it as it tiptoes up our creek. The fog shrouds Icebreaker and the dock and then the pier.

Mesmerized, I watch the low-rolling cloud approach the house, then cover the window with its gray haze. If

I didn't know what lay beyond, I would think the world had been wiped away by magic.

And now...at last...I sleep.

CHAPTER TWENTY-EIGHT

SRRTD

I awaken with the fog I had seen outside my window now inside my head. Disoriented and sluggish, I keep my eyes closed, taking in the faint sounds trickling in through my brain haze. A strange "beep...beep...beep" in the distance reminds me of the warning noise a construction vehicle makes when backing up. But that can't be.

The odors irritating my nose are familiar but out of place...an unsavory concoction of cleaners, disinfectants, ozone, latex, and rubbing alcohol. I've smelled them before, but long ago, and never in my cottage by the creek.

As my head clears, I'm able to grasp the meaning of the sounds and odors. Fear rides the wave of my growing comprehension. They are clinical in nature, and I'm scared I'll open my eyes and find I'm in a hospital. I hate hospitals. But I've not survived this long by being afraid. Straining to raise my heavy eyelids, the room slowly comes into view.

Though indistinct at first, I see someone sitting in a nearby chair dressed in scrubs. A late twenty-something African-American male. He lifts his gaze from the magazine he's holding and sees I've come around. Without taking his eyes off me, he leans toward the wall behind my bed and pushes a button.

"Yes?" a voice says, coming from a speaker I can't see.

"Hey, Donny, would you let Dr. Adams and Dr. Breckenridge know our patient is awake? Thanks."

"Will do," the voice affirms, followed by an electronic click ending the communication.

"How are you feeling?" the man asks while checking a monitor displaying my vital signs.

Instead of answering, I remain silent. I'm not volunteering anything about myself until I understand what's going on. In the background, I hear a staticky voice from a public address system call for doctors Adams and Breckenridge to "please report to the white room, stat."

"It's OK if you don't remember," scrubs says, "but my name is Marcus and I'm your personal nurse...well, most of the time. I've been taking good care of you."

"Personal nurse?" I ask. "We've met before? Why do I need a nurse?"

"All your questions will be answered once Dr. Adams and Dr. Breckinridge are here. I've been instructed not to provide any updates until–"

"And here we are," a professionally dressed woman with glasses interrupts as she enters the room. An older man wearing a white lab coat two-sizes too big and who looks like the old cartoon character Droopy follows on her heels. "Thank you, Marcus. You may leave for now, but don't go too far."

"This is Dr. Adams," the woman says, nodding her head toward Droopy. "And I'm Dr. Breckinridge. Dr. Adams is your physician and I'm your psychologist. We–"

"Psychologist!" I blurt out, straining to sit up. There's a bloody lot to figure out here, and the idea I need a psychologist is too much. "Where the heck am I, and why do I need a psychologist?"

The two doctors exchange a knowing look, like I've somehow confirmed their worst fears.

"Please," Dr. Droopy sighs, knotting his eyebrows. "Try not to interrupt. We know you have a lot of questions and we're going to answer them. In fact, if you'll let Dr. Breckinridge proceed unimpeded, she will tell you everything you need to know...everything we know...all at one time. It's a lot of information to take in, but we've agreed to try a different approach this time."

"This time?" I ask, my words laced with uncertainty.

"Listen closely," Dr. Breckenridge says, taking over. "This is the third time since we found you that you've come out of a coma. The previous two times we brought you along slowly...let you learn about who you are and how you got here a little at a time so as not to overwhelm you."

"We thought it was the right way to bring you back, to help you recover," Dr. Droopy says. "We were wrong. Both times you relapsed. We're not sure if it is attributable to physiological or psychological reasons. But...I've conducted every test I know and can't find anything wrong with you physically. So, while I have reservations about how effective a full memory immersion will be, I don't see any medical reason not to try it her way. Especially given the fact the first two times have failed to produce a permanent result."

"When I begin, you are not to interrupt me for any reason," Dr. Breckenridge says. "When I'm done, we will answer any and all questions you may have. If we don't know the answer to a question, we will tell you."

She pauses and takes a deep breath.

"Are you ready?"

"I...I guess," I say. My thoughts are scattered in a million directions. "Wait! No. I need a glass of water. Please."

"Of course," Dr. Breckenridge says, reaching into a small refrigerator on a countertop next to her. "Will bottled water be OK? It's cold."

"Yes. Please."

She breaks the cap's seal with a twist and hands me the bottle. I remove the cap and down most of the water in one long drink. My body absorbs the liquid like a sponge and I feel a little better.

"Hand me another one, will you?" I say, then down the rest of the bottle. I study her as she reaches into the fridge, then twists the second cap. She's a beautiful woman, but there's something off about her. She's too beautiful. Too...perfect. Her glasses make her look more professional than she would otherwise. Not that beautiful women can't be professionals. Such biases are a fact of modern life. The thing is, her lenses look like clear glass. A prop. But it's not just that.

"Now," Dr. Perfect Face says as I twist the cap back on the half-empty bottle. "Are you ready? And remember, no interruptions until I finish, OK?"

"OK," I say, nodding my head. I rest the bottle of water in my lap in case I need another drink.

"We call you Nadia," she begins. "No, it's not your real name. We don't know what your real name is. Nadia is the name of the hurricane associated with your accident. We thought the name Nadia was more personal than using Jane Doe.

"We found you about a week after the hurricane. You were unconscious in a house near the Neuse

River where a sailboat had come ashore. You had a head injury and were dehydrated. When you came out of the coma, you told us you had been befriended by a dog named Tonka. You claimed you had been living in the house, and that you had been on a quest to free all the pets trapped inside the surrounding houses. None of those things happened. The pets were never released and there is no dog named Tonka."

I'm not believing a word she says, but I don't interrupt. I want her to keep talking because I know she's going to get something wrong and I will expose her as the liar she is.

"It took us months to convince you those experiences had taken place in your subconscious. Your recovery was complicated by the shock you suffered when we told you about the...the Great Human Reset. The Great Reset is the euphemistic term we have given the event responsible for annihilating more than ninety-nine percent of the world's population."

"Ninety-nine percent is a conservative estimate," Dr. Adams interrupts. "Almost no one survived the cataclysmic event which coincided with the hurricane. Fortunately for you, Dr. Breckenridge and I and a handful of other medically trained people in the area survived and were able to care for you. But it hasn't been easy."

"We'll tell you more about the Reset later, as it is extremely technical," Dr. Perfect Face continues. "For now, suffice it to say mankind tried to play God with science, and science didn't like it."

"Or God didn't like it," Dr. Droopy says.

The psychologist adjusts her glasses, annoyed by Droopy's interruption, then resumes.

"As I said, the shock of learning almost everyone was dead set you back...triggered something inside you...and you lapsed into another coma lasting several more months. When you finally came to, we discovered you had been living an alternate life in your mind. You believed you had rescued a girl named Roxie from the river and the two of you had gone on various adventures and were creating a new life with the dog named Tonka. Again, we brought you along slowly, reintroducing you to reality while trying to guide you to the conclusion your memories were in fact coma-induced fantasies. It was a long, slow process. But after many therapy sessions and exercises in logic, you were coming around."

"That is, we *thought* you were coming around," Dr. Droopy interjects.

"You had another trigger experience," Dr. Perfect Face says, reclaiming control of the conversation before her colleague derailed the narrative. "It was the first time we took you out to see the town. We thought...or rather...I believed you were ready for outside stimulation. I believed you could handle seeing the world as it is instead of holding on to memories of how it used to be. It would have worked. It should have worked."

"Dr. Breckenridge underestimated just how profound the commitment to your fantasy world is," the physician says.

"Please!" the woman doctor says, unable to suppress her aggravation. "You are sabotaging the process I've laid out. I have to establish each layer of the history in a specific, straightforward way or the whole underpinning of her recovery will collapse and all of this will have been for nothing."

"My apologies," Dr. Droopy says, though he doesn't sound contrite at all. "Please, continue."

"It seems the attachment you have for this Westie, this Tonka, is ingrained in your psyche. Even after having convinced you all the things you experienced were false memories, you could not...would not...let go of the belief the dog is real. You claimed you had let go, and I believed you. But while we were in town, we came across a small, white terrier and you had a psychotic episode. A melt-down, if you will. Seeing the stray dog convinced you all of your memories were real. When I tried to persuade you otherwise...to bring you back to the level of awareness you were before seeing the dog...it was too much. It was like a rubber band snapping. You sank into another coma."

We stare at each other, waiting to see who will make the next move. Her eyes, muted by the reflections on her glasses, are both intense and uncertain. The way she has her dark hair pulled back behind her head gives her a stern, no-nonsense look and her mouth neither smiles nor frowns. She's all business. All science. And something isn't right about her. I just can't figure out what it is.

Dr. Adams, who looks like the stereotypical, middle-aged family practitioner, complete with graying temples and a stethoscope hanging around his shoulders, remains a quiet observer. He, too, is waiting. Studying me to see how I am going to react. But in his case, I think he's more interested in seeing how Dr. Breckenridge responds to my reaction than in anything having to do with my wellbeing or mental state.

"OK," I say, taking a deep breath. "So tell me…why is it I remember all the so-called fantasy things, but nothing about my time here with you? Shouldn't I be having a memory rush or something right now? You know, like in the movies when special effects make it look like the entire world is closing in on the main character? And she realizes everything she thought was true is false? And everything she thought was a lie is true?"

The two doctors eye each other, then the lady shrink lets out a knowing sigh.

"It's a condition called Stress-Related Reality Transference," she says, as though it's something she's repeating for the hundredth time. "Much like Post-Traumatic Stress, it can present itself either as a syndrome or a disorder. If it occurs immediately after a stress-related incident, it's considered a syndrome. If it occurs months or years after the incident, it is a disorder."

"Our theory," Dr. Droopy says, sensing it was a good time for him to jump back into the conversation, "is you suffered Stress-Related Reality Transference *Syndrome* because of the shock of living through a hurricane while under sail. Later, because the episode didn't heal on its own, it evolved into a disorder. It's possible the head injury you suffered at the same time somehow made the condition permanent. We don't really know."

"The important thing to understand is," Dr. Perfect Face continues, "in the attempt to make an intolerable reality manageable...your mind replaced reality with a fantasy. Something it could more easily deal with, where you became the hero. Able to save yourself and others, like the dog and the girl named Roxie. It is a self-preservation mechanism and, apparently, one so deeply entrenched in your psyche it is nearly impossible to cure."

"So..." I say, "you want me to believe, not only are Tonka and Roxie figments of my imagination, so are Charlotte, Goldie and Rebel? And everything we accomplished is a phony-bologna alternate reality? Is that what you expect me to believe?"

"I knew it!" Dr. Droopy says. "Her fantasy world expanded during the latest coma. Her condition isn't improving...it's growing worse."

"We planned for this," Dr. Perfect Face says calmly. Though her eyes are locked on mine, she speaks as though I'm not in the room. "We must activate Phase Two of the total immersion or the therapy will fail."

"You know my reservations," Droopy says. "Not only do I think it won't work, I believe it will send her into another coma. One from which she will never recover."

"Hey!" I shout at the two pointy-headed medical nerds. "What the actual suffering Hades are you doing? I'm sitting right here! Quit talking about me like I'm some kind of lab experiment! I want to know what you people are talking about...right now!"

"You're right," Dr. Perfect Face says. "My apologies. The fact is, there's no way this will work unless you fully understand what we are doing and we have your full consent to do it."

"Uh...do what?" I ask, not sure I want to know the answer.

"To do the one thing that will force you to accept reality. I want to take you home."

CHAPTER TWENTY-NINE

Homecoming

It's a short ride from the hospital...which isn't a hospital at all...to the marina downtown. As they escorted me to the van, I saw the building was really a small clinic or a former urgent care facility. It makes sense they've adapted it for their own purposes. The roof is covered with solar panels and the sound of a generator indicates they have alternative power for when the sun isn't out...like now. It's a cold, cloudy morning, and though it doesn't look like it will rain, there's no way the solar panels are generating much power.

When the van stops, Drs. Perfect Face and Droopy help me out the side door because I'm groggy and weak. I think they drugged me with something to make me sleep through the night. Marcus places his arm around my shoulder to steady me as we walk onto the main pier.

"Why don't we just take the van to the house?" I ask. I may be wobbly, but the cold is reviving me and my mind is working overtime to make sense of what's happening.

"Because the trees blown down by the hurricane still block the road," the nurse-turned-van-driver named Marcus, says. "The only way to get there is by water or air, and we don't have a helicopter. So..."

"But...we cleared the road," I say as Marcus helps me navigate the pier. "Roxie and I sawed a path through all the fallen trees wide enough to drive a motorcoach through. I know, because Charlotte drove hers through them."

"Your memory of clearing the road is another facet of your fantasy life," Dr. Perfect Face says. "We found evidence you tried cutting through a tree but gave up and left the chainsaw in the middle of the road. Your delusions have an element of truth, but are greatly exaggerated."

"I have a *lot* of memories," I say, still not buying her psychobabble. "When we get to the house, I'll prove my experiences were real. The one thing I don't understand is why you're trying to make me believe they aren't."

"I was wondering when you would try this argument again," Dr. Droopy says. "We explained all of this the previous two times you became cognizant."

"Let me be candid, Nadia," Dr. Breckenridge says.

"My name is Ivy!" My head reels from the exertion and Marcus tightens his grip for fear I'll fall off the pier into the water.

"We don't know how many other people survived the Reset," she continues, ignoring my outburst. "When Dr. Adams said there are a handful of other survivors in our group...he meant exactly that. Five. In addition to the three of us and Donny back at the clinic...our total number is nine. That's it."

Everyone is silent as we approach the powerboat waiting to take us downriver. Marcus climbs in first, then Droopy helps me over the gunwale into the boat. The male nurse grabs hold again and eases me down into a stern seat. Marcus takes the pilot's seat and starts the engine as the two doctors climb aboard. Droopy casts off the mooring lines and takes the passenger seat next to Marcus. Dr. Perfect Face settles into the seat across from me at the stern.

"It must have been hard to care for me while doing everything necessary to survive," I say as Marcus pilots the boat under the drawbridge. Off to the left, I see the park where I docked Icebreaker on my first visit. Ahead of us are the twin highrise bridges we'll pass under to go home.

"We were very fortunate," Perfect Face says, choosing each word. I think she knows I'm trying to set a trap...catch her in a lie. "The main hospital is also a disaster shelter and has almost all the supplies we need. We relocated to the clinic because it's smaller and easier to maintain. Less of a drain on power resources. If we run out of something, we can usually find it at the hospital. So, not only has it been easy to care for you, it gives us something useful to do. A way to apply our skills."

"But why didn't I see signs of you guys when I came to town searching for people?" I ask, pulling the down coat they gave me tighter.

Dr. Perfect Face studies me before answering, her eyes darting back and forth, trying to see behind my blank façade.

"Because you never came to town until we found you, remember?" she says. The turn at the corners of her mouth is almost imperceptible...almost. "The belief you came to New Bern is based on your fabricated memory, one we deconstructed last time. It's my hope this aspect of your recovery will resume once you see where we found you."

I remain quiet for the rest of the trip to conserve my strength and to make a plan for when I expose their lies. For some reason, they're going to extraordinary lengths to trick me, which means it's important to them. It also means I could be in grave danger when I expose them.

Though lost in my thoughts while gazing across the water, I become aware Dr. Breckenridge is studying me. Watching to see how I will react to the familiar landmarks we pass. Her hair is still pulled back, but now she's wearing one of those headband-earmuff things, that's both stylish and functional. The matching designer coat would have cost eight hundred dollars before The Great Reset, as they call it. Her thigh-high boots were meant to impress, not to protect her feet and legs from mud and briars like the combat boots they gave me to wear. If she was going for post-apocalypse chic...she nailed it.

The cold has given color to her cheeks she didn't have before, and the head wrap draws my gaze to her eyes. Once again, I'm struck by how perfect she is. She looks like something from a computer algorithm programed to determine what combinations of feminine features are most appealing. Then someone applied the results to the woman sitting across from me. She is aware of her beauty, but oblivious to the fact she is too pretty. Too perfect. She creeps me out.

"We have to dock at the marina because the creek behind the house is too shallow for this boat," Marcus says, as if I didn't know.

He turns the wheel to port and a couple of minutes later we dock next to the waterside cafe I took refuge in during a thunderstorm. As we step onto the dock, I see something familiar yet out of place. Moored in the boat slip where I found it floats Icebreaker.

"Wait!" I say, both excited and confused. "See the sailboat! It's the one I've been using since the hurricane. And look. Right on the stern, it says Titanic

II–Icebreaker. I don't know why it's here and not at the house, but it's my boat alright. Come on, I'll prove it."

To my surprise, instead of stopping me, they watch from the pier as I hop aboard. Ducking into the cabin, I go right to the navigation table where I keep the charts with my handwritten notes and the Captain's Log I've maintained...but they aren't there. Instead, I find the original charts and the logbook maintained by the boat's owner.

Stunned and confused, I sit on the edge of the berth to gather my thoughts. It must be some kind of ruse to convince me they're telling the truth. That I really did create an alternate reality. But it won't work. I won't let it work. And this time I'm thinking things through before reacting. It's a skill I've learned watching Charlotte, and I intend to put it to good use.

A quick visual scan of the cabin reveals nothing proving I was ever aboard this vessel, so I rummage through the drawers, cabinets, cubbyholes and nooks where I might find something they can't deny is mine. But after several minutes of searching, no joy. There are plenty of things I've used, but nothing connecting them to me and my reality. Then I remember something.

"OK," I say, stepping back outside onto the deck, "If this isn't my boat, how do I know about the repair work done on the port-side gunnel near the bow where I hit the dock? Look for yourself. I fixed the damage, but never got around to painting it."

They move up the dock a few feet to where they can see the boat's portside. Drs. Perfect Face and Droopy look at each other, then at me.

"I'll bring the golf cart to the end of the pier," Marcus says, then takes off toward the café.

"Well?" I say, dying to hear their lame explanations.

"Nadia...I mean...Ivy, look for yourself," Breckenridge says, gesturing toward the bow. "There's nothing wrong with the gunnel and it doesn't need painting."

Stepping up on the pilot's seat so I can look over the cabin, I can't believe my eyes. She's not lying. It's not a trick. The gunnel looks like it did before the accident. Like there had never been an accident. The paint where the damage should be is as faded as the rest of the boat. I look away, but not toward them. I won't let them see the sting in my eyes.

"It's alright," Dr. Perfect Face says, extending her hand to help me back onto the pier, and for a moment I almost believe the empathy in her voice is real. "Come on, the cart is waiting."

Marcus is waiting at the front of the café, sitting behind the wheel of a gas-powered golf cart I've never seen before, and I wonder how he found it so quick. The marina is part of a golfing community, so there are plenty of carts in the area. But still...

"Where did you find the wheels?" I ask, trying to sound casual as we climb into the cart.

"We were here for about a week before we found you," Dr. Droopy says. He takes the front passenger seat and turns to answer while Dr. Perfect Face and I sit next to each other in the back. "We came here to take advantage of the giant cell tower next to the café, but lightning had fried it. We found a couple of these carts at the marina's maintenance shed and recovered them to search for survivors. They're quite handy. We've used them several times since we found you, when we come back to look for equipment we can't find in town."

The cart is zipping through the resort community now. The puttering of the engine and the whirring of rubber tires on the asphalt are the only sounds we hear. Breckenridge continues to study my face for reactions as I survey the houses and vacation units we pass. It's all familiar to me, of course, but there's one big difference...none of the doors are open. I never bothered to come back and shut the ones I'd left open so pets could get out. There wasn't any reason to. Somebody must have closed them all, unless...such a thing never happened.

The thought mocks me. It's the first crack of doubt in the stone foundation of my belief my memories are real. The idea my life with Roxie and the Lost Girls never happened is too heartbreaking to accept. Yet...the proof the undamaged sailboat represents is impossible to ignore.

"Stop!" I shout as we pass a familiar house. Marcus hits the brakes, and I spring out of the cart as it skids to a stop. "This is the first place I broke into when I began looking for trapped pets. See the doorframe where the dead bold is? It's damaged. I did that!"

Drs. Perfect Face and Droopy join me at the entryway, but instead of looking guilty or concerned, their faces are a mix of pain and pity.

"Look!" I say, opening the door. "Here, in the foyer. There's one of those piles of silica, and I stepped right in the middle–"

I stop short because the pile isn't there. Instead, the sand-like substance is spread all over the floor. Boot prints left by several people can be seen in the remaining dust.

"We've been in almost all these houses," Droopy says, placing his hand on my shoulder. "We had to break into the ones that were locked."

"I don't believe you," I say, continuing to stare at the floor, but the crack in my foundation grows wider.

"Come," Breckenridge says, taking me by the arm and leading me outside. "We're almost there."

A minute later we turn onto Shadow Lane and I see the house where I've lived for more than a year...but everything looks different. The gardens we planted and the animal pens we built are gone. In their place is a single row scratched in the dirt and a few boards, perhaps for building a chicken coop. In the wooded lot next to Tonka's house are the remains of a beehive, its various sections scattered about as though it had come apart during the flood.

"You were on your own for several weeks before we found you," Dr. Perfect Face says. She's standing behind me where I can't see her. "You were surviving, but in a state of extended shock. Your mental condition had deteriorated to the point you were delusional.

"As I said earlier, there's a grain of truth to most of the fantasies you've created. Instead of a thriving farm with multiple gardens and livestock, you had scratched a hole in the dirt and nailed a few boards together. *This* is what I wanted you to see. *This* is your reality."

"But...Tonka?" I whisper, refusing to believe he exists only in my imagination. "He was real. He had to be real. I wouldn't have survived without him."

"Indeed," Dr. Breckenridge says, her tone conveying neither affirmation nor disagreement. "Let's go into the house."

Everything looks the same to me as Breckenridge, Adams and I climb the steps to the front door. The same...but somehow...off. Droopy opens the door and when I step inside, a rush of "home" sweeps over me. The furniture and artwork on the walls, everything is as I remember it. But again, something isn't right.

The house looks like it hasn't been lived in for some time. Empty water bottles litter the kitchen countertop, the trashcan in the corner is overflowing, cleaned dishes are stacked beside the sink, never put away. It appears someone lived here for a few days, then left in a hurry. But there's something else. No lights or fans are on and the familiar hum of the refrigerator is gone.

"Why is the power off?" I ask. "Did something happen to the solar panels?"

"Solar panels?" Dr. Droopy says. "There are no solar panels. This house lost power at the same time the others did."

Without thinking, I reach for the refrigerator door to look inside...to prove to myself he's lying.

"I wouldn't do that!" Perfect Face warns, but I ignore her and open the door.

A putrid stench hits me like a brick to the face, and I gag. Shoving the door closed, I rush to the kitchen sink just in case I lose my breakfast. The nausea passes, and I look at Breckenridge.

"Had enough?" she says, forcing her expression and voice to remain neutral. But her eyes can't hide the triumph she's enjoying.

"What's today's date?" I ask. The question squashes her little mental victory dance, but she answers anyway.

"January the twelfth," she says without asking why I want to know.

Simple math tells me...if I was here on Christmas Day as I remember...they had over two weeks to remove evidence of the changes we'd made and of Tonka, Roxie and the Lost Girls. They had time to make Icebreaker look undamaged, to walk through houses I had broken into, and to rework everything in and around Tonka's house so it looks abandoned. I don't know why they would try to fool me, but it is possible.

Even as the thought forms in my head, my logical brain tags the idea as desperation. That I'm clutching at straws to maintain a belief outside of reasonable explanation. The crack in my foundation grows wider still.

Breckenridge and Adams remain silent as I walk through the other rooms, still hoping to find evidence my memories are real. I don't bother going upstairs to the computer...because there is no power. There's no way to turn it on and show them the dozens of new files Roxie and I created.

Instead, I head to the main bedroom to show them the automatic I keep on top of the nightstand. But when I step inside the room, I stop! Instead of my handgun, sitting on the nightstand is a five-by-seven, framed photograph of a West Highland Terrier. Tonka. The room spins around me. I have to sit on the edge of the bed for fear of collapsing. When I look up, I see the wall opposite the bed is filled with photographs of Tonka. They show him as a puppy and when he was being trained and as a show dog. The entire wall is a shrine to the Westie, filled with pictures I've never seen.

The foundation of who I believe myself to be shatters into a million pieces. Tears stream down my cheeks, but I refuse to sob. If the facts are irrefutable, I have no choice but to concede Dr. Breckenridge is telling the truth. That I really did create a fantasy life.

Then, like a small ember glowing beneath the ashes, a thought occurs to me. I still have no memories of her version of who I am or what's happened since the storm! It's not proof she's right, it's a lack of proof I'm wrong. It's the last spark connecting me to a life I want to believe is real. I won't let it die until I can recall memories supporting her story of who I am.

"I know this is very difficult for you," Dr. Perfect Face says as she sits next to me on the bed. "It may seem cruel, but you had to see for yourself. I'm convinced it's the only way to bring you back to reality and to make it stick this time."

"I have to go for a walk," I say, leaving her on the bed.

"Of course," I hear her say as I descend the interior stairway exiting under the house. "Take all the time you need. Dr. Adams and I will wait for you."

The air is icy and a brisk wind stings my eyes. I can hear the two of them talking...about me, I'm sure...but I don't care.

What matters is that you continue to believe in yourself, the little voice inside my head says. It's been a long time since I've heard my inner voice. It's been a long time since I've needed to hear it.

Thinking more calmly now, a new idea presents itself. Although Icebreaker isn't here, there may be evidence it had been, or a clue as to who removed it. If this is all a trick, they've done a bang-up job of it. It's doubtful they made a mistake or missed something that reveals the villain behind the mask...you know, like every episode of Scooby-Doo ever. But I still don't remember the things they say I'm supposed to, so there's no way I'm letting go of the thread tethering me to my version of what's happened.

When I reach the end of the pier, there's nothing. Not even a mooring line or a scuff mark where I hit the dock with Icebreaker. Even the chairs Roxie and I sat in to observe the stars are gone. Nothing.

Disheartened, I sit on the edge of the dock and stare into the creek. The water is clear and I can see a pair of mullet skimming the bottom for detritus. If Tonka was with me, he would bark at them. The wind gusts and I sink lower into my coat, struggling to hold back tears. I've never been more alone in my life...at least the life I remember. I don't know what my former life was like, and right now, I don't want to know. I want Tonka and my friends. I want things to be like they were.

"You doing OK?" Dr. Perfect Face asks. I've been so lost in my thoughts I didn't hear the heavy soles of her boots on the wood planks. "You've been out here for an hour. We were becoming a little concerned and came to check on you. Sorry to disturb you."

I look over my shoulder to see them standing side-by-side at the point the pier connects to the dock. They're overdressed, out of place, and annoyed at having to stand in the cold. I stand and turn to face them, wishing they would just disappear.

"I know you're close to accepting the truth," Breckenridge says, locking her flawless eyes on mine. The woman may have sacrificed some luxuries because of the apocalypse, but makeup isn't one of them. "We'll stay here all day if we have to because we don't want to lose you again. I truly believe if you lapse into another coma, you will die. You won't come back. We need you."

And there it is. The unformed question hiding in the shadows of my subconsciousness now flails about like one of those inflatable tube men you see on used car lots.

"Why?" I say, moving closer. "What do you need me for? You don't need me to help you survive. You don't need me to help you with medical things. As far as I can tell, you don't need me for anything."

"Well...it's...you don't–"

"Stop!" I say, cutting her off. I know whatever follows is going to be a load of bovine excrement. "I couldn't put my finger on it before, but now...now I know what's wrong. You're not helping me because you're good Samaritans trying to save a sick girl. You're helping me because you want me for something. You need me for something. I just don't know what it is."

"I told you it wouldn't work," Droopy says, though now I'm not sure whether he's talking about Dr. Breckenridge's therapy or their scam. "Her mind is...too strong."

"No!" Breckenridge says. "We're *so* close. Ivy, you must listen to me. You did this last time and we almost lost you. You have to believe me."

"You know what..." I say, stepping closer. "I don't believe a–"

The unspoken words hang in the air as my brain struggles to grasp the truth of what my eyes see in the marsh. There, just off to the side of the pier, lodged between two clumps of cattails and partially covered by mud...is Tonka's green, dumbbell-shaped squeaky toy.

CHAPTER THIRTY

Journey

Breckenridge follows my gaze and spots the toy in the mud. Panic washes across her face. She knows I see through their elaborate deception. As she turns her eyes back to me, the panic on her face morphs into anger.

She opens her mouth to say something, but I'm done with their lies. I throw my weight into her upper body, catching her off-guard, knocking her off the pier. She lands face first in the mud with a very satisfying plop.

Turning just in time to see Droopy coming at me, I duck and spin, executing a perfect leg sweep. *Thank you, martial arts training, wherever you come from!* The doctor lands flat on his back, knocking the wind out of him. I grab his ankles and swing his legs toward the edge of the pier with all the force I can muster. Where the legs go, the body must follow. Into the marsh he goes.

I glance over to check on Breckenridge and see she's grabbed the edge of the planking, trying to climb back up. Not a simple task when you're standing in mud and the pier is as high as your shoulders. Still, I want to keep her from following me as long as possible, so I stomp her left hand with my heavy combat boot. The crunch I hear is even more satisfying than the plopping sound was.

"That should slow you down a while," I say, though I don't think she hears because she's screaming and cussing so loud. Oh, well...sucks to be you!

Her cries of agony follow me as I run down the pier. If Marcus hears the commotion, he'll come to see what's happening. But it's a long pier, and nurse dude is on the far side of the house.

Downshifting into a fast walk as I approach the end of the pier, I try to catch my breath and calm myself. As far as Marcus knows, everything is fine. I don't want to give him any reason to think otherwise. I need the element of surprise if I'm going to make it past this big guy.

"Hey," I say as I emerge from under the raised house. The nurse-minion is leaning against the golf cart, smoking a cigarette, oblivious to what happened out on the dock.

"Alright!" he says, no doubt bored out of his mind. "You guys ready to go?"

"Yeah," I say. "Dr. Perfect Face and Dr. Droopy will be here in a minute."

"Perfect Face and Droopy," he repeats, chuckling. "Priceless. I think you nailed them."

"More than you know," I say with too much glee.

"So, tell me, have you figured out the truth about Dr. Breckenridge yet?"

I'm focused on my next moves, so I'm not sure if he means the con game she's been pulling or something else. It doesn't matter.

"Wait..." he says, tossing the cigarette on the gravel driveway and crushing it with the toe of his shoe. "Do you hear someone yelling?"

I know what I'm about to do isn't a cool Krav Maga move or anything like that, but I know it'll work.

"Look, a wasp! I say, extending my left hand toward his face.

He lifts his chin just like I knew he would, and I punch him in the throat. He bends over, coughing and gasping, so I kick him in the groin from behind and he falls to the ground. I'm really loving these heavy boots.

The wheels of the cart throw gravel in his face as I speed off toward the marina. He's still yelling a stream of profanities as I turn the corner. I don't blame him. That's gotta hurt.

Arriving at the marina, I blow through the parking lot and keep going. The wood planks groan under the weight of the golf cart as I drive over the pier to the powerboat. Any other time, I'd be worried the planks might break. Heck, any other time I wouldn't be driving the cart on the pier. But I'm not wasting a moment getting out of here. I'm *not* going to give them a chance to catch me.

I cast off the mooring lines, jump into the boat, and fire up the twin outboard engines. Signs that say NO WAKE are posted all over the place...but, hey! Who cares? This is the apocalypse. I make my own rules.

"Surf's up!" I yell as I gun the engines.

Two minutes later, I stop in the middle of the Neuse, realizing I don't know whether I should go upriver or downriver. That's me again all over. All action, no planning. Time to think things through.

As the boat drifts with the river, I look toward New Bern. It doesn't make sense to go there. Droopy and Perfect Face will go back at some point. I could go farther upriver, past town. Maybe even make it to Kinston. But I don't know the area. Rebel would know her way around, but she's not here.

The thought of Rebel leads me to thinking of the other girls and Tonka. They have to be somewhere. For all I know, they were in town, too. Heck, they could have been in the same building I was and I wouldn't have known. The only room I saw was mine.

But I don't know if they were captured by the Med Team Mafia, as I've started thinking of them. They may have gotten away when the fog came. They could be anywhere. If they escaped, where would they go? Where would I have gone?

A new thought hits me like a Rowdy Ronda Rousey roundhouse. *Seriously, my memory burps come in alliterations now?* If Roxie is leading the Lost Girls, they probably went to Cherry Point...the place she knows best. It's easy to reach by water and...there's another reason to go there. A big reason.

It's amazing how much faster a powerboat is than a sailboat. That may sound like a "no duh" kind of observation, but I haven't moved this fast since...I don't know when. But it's fast!

In what seems like twenty nanoseconds, I'm beaching the boat at the general's house where Roxie watched for passing vessels. As I dash inside, I figure there has to be a base directory with important telephone numbers somewhere. And, it may have a street map inside with important facilities highlighted.

I don't know if the Med Team Mafia is coming after me yet. I don't even know if they saw which way I went. But it feels like I'm running out of time, so I tear through drawers and cabinets like the Kardashians with unlimited credit cards shopping for cosmetics. After about two minutes, I open a drawer containing a bunch of takeout menus, appliance warranties and...VOILA!...a base directory with a street map on the third page. I'm in like Flynn...whoever he is.

My eyes scan the various street names on the map at warp speed until I find Cryogenics Road...the one

Roxie mentioned on the dock when we were stargazing. I rip the map page out of the directory, dash out the front door and begin jogging through the base.

As I make my way through the intersecting streets, I keep an eye out for Tonka, Roxie, and the others. No joy. No signs of them at all. It's disappointing, but at the moment I have a bigger objective. I'll figure out where they are later.

In what seems like hours, but is only minutes, I stop at the end of Cryogenics Road in front of a huge, white, square building, three-stories high with dozens of antennas and satellite dishes on its roof and surrounding lots. As I open the door, I hear the drone of an engine off in the distance. Pausing, I strain to listen...but whatever it was is gone. If it existed at all.

The lights come on when I enter, triggered by a motion sensor, I'm sure. So the building must have an emergency power system. A very robust one if it's lasted this long. It makes sense, though. If this building does what I think it does, it has to maintain power. The consequences of a power outage would have been devastating.

I give the interior a quick scan and...YES!. My lucky streak is on a roll. Everything in the building is clearly marked. Signs over the doors have titles like WHITE HOUSE, PENTAGON, NORAD, NATO, CIA, FEMA, DCGS and a bunch of other acronyms. But there's only one acronym I'm interested in...the one that says NASA...the National Aeronautics and Space Administration.

This will save a lot of time. I don't have to go to each floor and check every room. A directory on the wall next to the elevator lists everything in the building. And there it is on the top floor...NASA Communication Center, Room 301.

It may seem like overkill, but I'm sure every major military facility in the country has a building like this. They're part of a redundancy, so no matter what happens...whether it be an act of war or a natural catastrophic event...essential civilian and military leaders can continue to communicate with each other. Or could have, if they were alive.

When the elevator door opens, I see Room 301 occupies the entire third floor. There's electronic equipment everywhere, with dozens of communication systems and giant TV screens on every wall. It looks a lot like the command centers they used to show on television whenever a rocket was launched.

A sign in the far corner of the room says, "Military Strategic Command and Control Communications." My suppressed memory must not retain information about the military. I'm not having one of those random memory eruptions these type situations bring on. But the facility's purpose is obvious. The modern military depends on communication satellites and GPS navigation. They can even control military equipment on the other side of the globe. It's the reason the U.S. Space Force was created. It's sort of like SkyNet in the

Terminator movies. But it's the other corner of the room I'm interested in. The one with the sign that reads, INTERNATIONAL SPACE STATION.

I'm careful not to step in the silica piles littering the room...because they're, you know, people...and wind my way around the various consoles and workstations to the ISS corner. It's easy to figure out which position is used for communicating with the space station. There's a bank of monitors on the wall with a sign above them that reads, ISS COMMUNICATIONS. If only everything in life was this easy.

I see silica in the seat behind the console, so I switch it with a clean chair and sit down. I slip the communication headgear over my head and flip the switch marked ISS. All twelve monitors stutter-flash on and...PEOPLE! I SEE PEOPLE! There are astronauts in various sections of the space station doing whatever astronauts do, but they're oblivious to me. They don't know I see them.

There are several Push To Talk buttons on the earpieces of the headset, so I push each one in succession, calling out, "Hello! Can you hear me? Anybody on the ISS, please respond." When I hit the third button, I see a man jump and look toward the camera marked Monitor Number One. He pushes off the wall, floats over to the camera and flips a switch. I can tell by his reaction his monitor is on and he can see me. Before he speaks, his expression changes from shock to...recognition?

"Oh my god!" he says, his hoarse voice cracking. "It can't be! Journey Steele, is that really you? We thought you were dead. We thought everyone was dead!"

"You...you know my name?" the voice coming from my mouth is sharp and breathless. The astronauts visible on the other monitors hear us and move at once to various comm stations throughout the ISS.

"Of course I know your name, goofus! You're the most famous teenager on earth. Everybody knows your name."

"But...how? Why? I don't–"

"Wait!" he says, cutting me off. "There's somebody here who's really gonna want to talk to you. Commander! Are you seeing–"

"Journey!" a woman's voice interrupts. "It's me! Look at camera six!"

I shift my focus to the monitor marked Number Six and see a woman astronaut with crazy floating hair staring at me, her expression an impossible mix of disbelief, relief and joy.

"Thank God you're alive!" she says, tears flowing down her cheeks.

"Who are you?" I ask, trying to make sense of everything that's happening. "How do you know who I am?

"Journey," the commander says, a cloud of concern spreading across her face. "It's me, your mother. Mom."

"Mom?"

—To Be Continued—

A Personal Request by the Author

The success of independently published writers such as myself is almost totally dependent on reader reviews. If you enjoyed this novel and would like to see more of my stories make it to print, please post a review on GoodReads.com, Amazon.com/books, Kindle.com, Audible.com, or other book-related websites. And please be sure to tell your friends. Thank you.

Other Books by W.C. Furney

Black Hearts White Bones
Aphrodite's Whisper

To learn more about W.C. Furney, visit his website.
www.billfurney.com